The Uist Girl Series Book 1

NO SONG
IN A
STRANGE LAND

An emotional and thought-provoking historical novel

MARION MACDONALD

Independently Published.

ISBN – 9798754837836

In memory of my grandparents
Angus and Marion

Author's Note

Last year, after finishing The Circle, I decided to research my family tree as I had time on my hands and no idea of what I would write about next. I'm glad I did, as *No Song in a Strange Land* would not have happened otherwise.

I found out that my grandfather, Angus Macdonald, had left North Uist to go to Canada in 1896 and had promised to come back and marry my grandmother, Marion, also Macdonald, when she grew up. He was twenty years older than her. True to his word he returned in 1911, they married and travelled to Canada to his farm in Saskatchewan. My dad's sister was born there, and I was told was delivered by a native woman. The wolves that howled in the night terrified my grandmother and she persuaded my grandfather to return to Scotland.

The initial idea for this book came from what I thought was a strange marriage arrangement between my grandparents. I never found out the reason for it, so everything in this book is from my imagination and bears no relation to whatever the reality of the situation was.

I thoroughly enjoyed the research that I carried out as I learned so much about life in the prairies and about World War 1. What a brave and adventurous generation they were. May we always remember them.

"How shall we sing the LORD's song in a strange land?"

From Psalm 137
The Holy Bible, King James Version

"Tha 'n talamh leir mun cuairt dhiom
'N mheallan suas 's na neoil
Aig na'shells' a'bualadh
Cha leir dhomh bhuam le ceo
Gun chlasneachd aig mo chluasan
Le fuaim a'ghunna mhoir"

"All the ground around me
Is like the hail in the heavens
With the shells exploding
I am blinded by smoke
My ears are deafened
By the roar of the cannon"

From An Eala Bhan – the White Swan
By Domhnall Ruadh Choruna (Donald MacDonald)
WW1 Poet from North Uist

PROLOGUE

The Factor's House, Lochmaddy, North Uist, 1920

As I gaze at his body lying in full military uniform inside the polished oak coffin, I can't help but smile at the irony of it all. Four years of fighting on the Western Front, but it was the influenza that had got him in the end. His body is being moved to Glasgow today so that he can be buried in the family plot with his father. Mrs McAllister had asked the undertaker to set the coffin up in the library to allow people to pay their respects. I was one of the few who had come. There weren't many people who had much respect for Colin Donaldson, and part of me was sad about that. I touch the small pink scar beneath his eye, which had not detracted from his handsome features, but knew he had unseen scars that had robbed him of more than his good looks.

I remember the day I met Colin. It was in this very room. I was sixteen and had just began working as a companion to his sister Victoria, who had polio and couldn't walk. We were sitting at the table where his casket now rests, playing a game of dominoes, when he burst through the door, making me drop my tiles.

'Victoria, I'm home,' he said, rushing over and embracing her. Victoria's face lit up with joy as she introduced her brother to me.

'This is my brother, Colin. He's been at the University of Glasgow but is joining us for the holidays. What fun we shall have,' she said, clasping her hands in excitement.

He was handsome, with floppy blond hair tumbling over his intense blue eyes, which then alighted on me. I felt my cheeks grow warm and looked down at my hands, which were trying to gather up my tiles.

'And who is this lovely young lady?'

'This is Chrissie, my friend and companion. You make sure you are kind to her, Colin. I don't want to lose her.'

'I shall indeed be kind to her,' he said, smiling at me in a way I had never been smiled at before. My sixteen-year-old heart quivered with pleasure and the seed of a dream that we would marry one day was sown.

The ghost of the girl I used to be giggles at my foolish dreams of marrying Colin Donaldson and becoming the mistress of this house one day. Yet, all these years later, that is what I am to become. I think about life and the twists and turns of my journey to Canada and back that have led to this. It all started just before I turned twenty and that letter from Roderick Macdonald arrived in the post.

CHRISSIE'S JOURNEY

North Uist 1910

CHAPTER ONE

The day the letter arrived was like any other January day. I awoke to the sound of my mother calling me to get up and to the familiar smells of peat smoke, oatmeal cooking on the fire and the stink from the animals that were brought inside in the winter.

'Christian,' Mother called, 'it's time to get up or you'll be late for work. Before you go, the pot needs emptying, and the cow needs milking.'

'Coming *Mathair*,' I called back, reluctantly leaving the warmth of the bed I shared with my sister Morag. Mother only called me Christian when she was giving me a warning, so I knew I shouldn't dawdle. My grandmother, who had lived with us until she died a couple of years ago, was named Christian so my parents had shortened my name to Chrissie to avoid confusion.

I washed my face with the warm water Mother had poured into the bowl on top of the chest of drawers then put on my skirt and blouse. Roughly pulling the brush through my curly fair hair with one hand, I poked Morag with my other hand as my sister was still lying sleeping, seemingly oblivious to Mother's call. I had to coax her out of bed every day. My father and my brothers, Lachlan and Johnny, were already up and out for their work on the croft. I then went through the curtain, pulled my shawl around me, and gingerly picked up the pot, making sure I didn't spill any of its contents until I reached the outhouse which reeked as much as the animals. Oh, for one of the new-fangled water closets they had recently installed up at the Factor's house that flushed everything away.

I breathed in the cold winter air and wished it were spring. I hated the winter. It was always so cold and wild on the island that I inevitably ended up with chilblains on my hands, which stung like the tawse from the teacher at school when I spoke the Gaelic. It was a working day, so I would walk with my sister to school and then make the mile walk to the big house where I worked. I was a part-time companion to Victoria Donaldson, the daughter of

6

Malcolm Donaldson, who looked after the estate on North Uist for the Laird. I had got the job as I could read, write, and talk fluently in the English, something that few other girls on the island could do. Gaelic was the language of the islands and although the government had tried to get rid of it by insisting that only English was taught in island schools, the islanders still spoke mostly in Gaelic.

Although we spoke the Gaelic to our neighbours, my father saw the benefits of speaking the language of the Laird and encouraged us to cultivate our English, so we spoke a mix of Gaelic and English at home. It was one of the ways we islanders could have more say over what happened to us he said. My father was always going on about how badly treated the crofters had been by the Laird, especially during the famine, and talked at length of how my grandfather and grandmother had helped to get the law changed in 1886 to give crofters more rights. From the way he talked, it was as if they had done it single-handed. But I hated when he and Mother went on about how hard life had been, as they made me feel anxious about my future. What if I couldn't marry someone with land or money? Like my forebears, it could leave me penniless and homeless.

'Morning, Chrissie,' Mother said, laying out a plate of porridge on the table.

'Morning *Mathair*.'

'The post is coming today,' Mother said, smiling with excitement at me.

I smiled back. Weather allowing, the steamers from the mainland that circulated around the islands delivered the mail to the post office in Lochmaddy once a week. It brought not only mail but newspapers and magazines that kept the islanders in touch with what was happening in the outside world. The Postmaster oversaw the distribution of the mail, and he organised it in such a way that he made a delivery once a week to each of the outlying districts. Although I was sure there would be nothing for me, it was

7

always a thrill waiting in anticipation for the mail carrier to call. It broke up the boring routine of our lives.

Sometimes there would be a letter from my Aunt Katie, who had moved to Glasgow. She worked as a clerk in the Scottish Co-operative Society and had joined the women's suffrage movement. Mother and I loved to hear about her life in the city, which to me was so much more exciting than on North Uist. At other times, it would be an official letter from the Laird and that wasn't so welcome as it might bring news of an increase in the rent for the croft.

'Oh, I hope there's a letter from Aunt Katie. She makes everything sound so interesting. I wonder if there'll be fresh magazines at the house today. Victoria and I just love looking at the latest fashions.'

'Fashion, is that all you can think about, my girl? There are much more important issues to be thinking about.'

'You mean like votes for women, *Mathair*? I don't know why you and Aunt Katie think it's so important. *Athair* has the vote and I like that it will be the role of my husband, whoever he may be, to cast his vote in whatever way best serves our family, just like him.'

'I don't understand how you can think like that. You certainly didn't get your silly ideas from me or your *Athair*. Sure, weren't your own grandparents involved in fighting for greater rights for crofters barely thirty years ago. It was only because of them he could get the vote.'

Here we go again, I thought, feeling the familiar knot in my stomach. Not that I ever let Mother know how I felt, so I just shrugged and went off to work. I much preferred to think about boyfriends and fashion rather than what might happen to me in the future. Not that I had a boyfriend, but I felt that the son of the house where I worked was sweet on me. When he was at home, Master Colin was forever creeping up behind me and one day when I was hanging up some washing for Miss Victoria, he even put his arms around my waist. He gave me such a shock I dropped the washing

8

basket, and the laundry had to be washed all over again. Mrs McAllister, the housekeeper, had been furious with me but despite this my heart was aflutter the entire day when I thought about him.

CHAPTER TWO

After I had walked with Morag to school, I made my way up to my place of work. It was a proper house built of stone with slates on the roof and was much grander than the black house that I lived in. Victoria had a nurse who helped with most of her bathing and toileting, but my job was to keep her company and entertain her during the day. We would look at the latest fashions in the women's magazines that she had delivered from the mainland, play games, read the novels of Jane Austen and the Brontës as well as have long discussions about romance and marriage. We were the same age, and I felt we were friends rather than mistress and maid.

'Good morning Chrissie,' said Janet, the housemaid. She had been my best friend at school, so we were delighted to be working together.

'Good morning, Janet. It is so cold today, isn't it?' I said, still wishing it were springtime. The only good thing about the winter was that there were no midges to nip the life out of you.

'Come on into the kitchen and heat yourself at the fire,' said Janet, 'and I'll get you a cup of tea.'

Janet was a live-in maid, and although she complained about the early rise to set and light the fires and serve breakfast, I knew she was happier here than with her own family. She was one of seven, so it was a treat having a room that she only had to share with one other person. I spotted the newspapers lying on the kitchen table and went over to have a look, but Janet stopped me in my tracks.

'Don't touch those papers. They're for the Master and he likes them to be nice, neat and untouched by human hand.'

'I only want a peak to see if there is anything of interest.'

'Well, you can't have one,' Janet said, scooping up the papers and taking them to safety.

As we drank our tea, we gossiped about what was going on.

'Did you hear that the Reverend McEwan had to visit Sheona Macqueen's parents, and it looks like there's going to be a wedding soon.'

'Who's the lucky husband?'

'I don't know but I heard a rumour that your brother Johnny was dancing a lot with her at the ceilidh last month.'

'No! *Mathair* and *Athair* will be so cross if he has done anything to bring shame on the family.'

'I'm only joking. I don't know who the father is.'

'Poor Sheona. If whoever the father is does not marry her, she will be shunned and might have to go into the workhouse.'

The door swung open, and we both stood up as Mrs McAllister came bustling into the kitchen.

'What are you two gossiping about? Nothing good, I expect. Miss Victoria is waiting for you Chrissie, so you better get up there. And you, Janet, get on with your work. There's a pile of ironing to do and vegetables to prepare for the lunch when you've finished.'

The day passed quickly, and I left after giving Miss Victoria her afternoon tea. When I set off, I noticed Master Colin following me and stopped.

'Why are you following me, Master Colin?'

'I really like you Chrissie and wonder if I could have a kiss.'

I hesitated and then offered my cheek, but before I knew what was happening, he was grasping me tightly to him and pressing his lips against mine. I found my body yielding to his embrace until a picture of the Reverend McEwan and the story that my friend Janet had told me about Sheona Macqueen came into my mind. Pulling away from him, I ran all the way home, frightened by my own feelings and what Master Colin had done. However, I couldn't help thinking how my life could change if he were to become my husband.

When I arrived home, I was surprised to see Father sitting beside Mother and Morag at the kitchen table.

'Sit down Chrissie, your *Athair* and I have something to tell you. Morag, go out and play just now.'

11

'I'm nearly fourteen *Mathair*, I don't play like a child anymore and besides, I've only just come home and I'm hungry.'

'Do as your *Mathair* tells you.'

Morag didn't need a second telling. She knew when our father would brook no nonsense.

'What's wrong? Why are you home early and looking so serious, *Athair*?'

My thoughts went back to Colin. Had Father somehow found out about Colin's kiss? I was sure to get a visit from the minister if he had.

'A letter came today, Chrissie,' Mother said.

'Oh, from Aunt Katie. What did she have to say? Can I read it?'

'It's not from your Aunt Katie,' Father continued the conversation. 'Do you remember I told you about my friend, Roderick Macdonald, who went to Canada?'

'Yes. I remember. He used to brush my hair when I was little, and I even asked him to marry me when I grew up. Silly girl that I was.'

I laughed at this, but then noticed that no one else was laughing.

'Well, the letter was from him. He's coming back to Scotland.'

'That will be nice for you, *Athair*, to see your old friend. But why are you looking so dour?'

'He's not coming home to see me. He's coming home to marry you.'

'To marry me?'

'Yes. Before he left for Canada, your *Mathair* and I promised that he could have your hand in marriage if he made a good life for himself in Canada. He has a farm in Saskatchewan now and is coming home to claim you for his bride as we said he could.'

'We didn't think he would keep us to our pledge,' Mother butted in. 'We thought that once he moved to Canada, he wouldn't give you a second thought.'

'But now that he's on his way home, we must honour our promise to him,' Father continued.

12

'Your promise! What kind of parents promise their daughter to a man who is old enough to be her father, to a man she hardly knows?'

I was outraged and jumped to my feet.

'I know it will be hard for me to find a suitable husband because of all the young men going over the Minch to the mainland but, promising me to this Roderick without my consent is going too far. It's a new century, for goodness' sake, and women are fighting to become more than just possessions.'

I could see Mother smiling at my reference to the conversation we had had that morning about the suffragettes. This made me even angrier, and my voice rose to a screech.

'I know I hate living in this black house, but I don't hate it enough to give up everything and everyone I love to live with a stranger in Canada.'

'Going to Canada will give you a chance at a whole new life where you won't be beholden to the Laird and his ilk,' Father said.

'It's your duty, Chrissie,' Mother interceded, appealing to my sense of responsibility. 'We agreed to Roderick's proposal, and he is making this long and arduous journey over the Atlantic to keep his side of the bargain. You will dishonour our family if you don't go through with it.'

'But Master Colin kissed me today, and that means he wants to marry me, doesn't it?' I blurted out, clutching at any straw to make what was happening stop. 'I don't want to marry this Roderick Macdonald. I want to marry Colin,' I wailed.

'You stupid child. Don't you know people like the Laird and his agents only use local girls for their own pleasure, not to marry them. They stick with their own class. You better not have gone further than kissing my girl or you'll feel the sting of my belt.'

At that, I burst into tears and rushed blindly into the bedroom. I felt as if my world was tumbling down, and I had no power to stop it.

CHAPTER THREE

I lay face down on my bed sobbing so didn't hear Mother come in until I felt her hand patting me softly on the back. This was something she used to do when I was a child and upset about something. I had always found it comforting and realised it still was. I turned around to look at Mother, who wiped away my tears with a clean handkerchief.

'There, there *mo ghraidh*,' she said, using the words she used for us when we were children. It was nice to feel like a child again, with no responsibilities.

'I'm sorry, *Mathair*, that I made such a fuss. It has just been a strange day. Master Colin kissing me like that frightened me and excited me at the same time. I know I was silly to think that he would want to marry me, but it is nice to have a dream.'

'I know Chrissie, but the upper classes stick with their own, and so do we. Master Colin did nothing more than just kiss you, did he?'

Fortunately, I could answer no to her question, but I knew I would have said no anyway, as the look of fear and disappointment on her face made me squirm with shame.

'I know Roderick is older than you would like,' she continued, 'but it means that he is more mature and that he has the income to take care of you. Remember on the islands, it's not unusual to have an older husband. Your grandmother, Christian, was twenty years younger than your grandfather and they were happy, so you and Roderick could be too. Here is his letter and a photograph of him. Have a look at that and come through when you are ready.'

'Thank you, *Mathair*,' I smiled wanly at her and blew my nose loudly into the now soggy handkerchief.

I looked at the envelope which Roderick had addressed to my father and pulled out a letter and a piece of paper with the image of a man on it. Roderick had written his letter in English, and his writing was easy to read.

Dear Angus,

I understand that you and my father have been discussing the arrangement that you and I came to about your daughter Chrissie, so I expect that this letter will not be a complete surprise to you. It has been 15 years since I last saw you and you promised your daughter to me when I had made my fortune and she was of an age to marry. I have not quite made my fortune, but I do own a farm and have built a house that is too big for a man on his own. I hope you have told her about our agreement and that she will not be too surprised when she hears of my intention to return and marry her.

I am enclosing a photograph of me so that she will know what I look like, and I hope she will not find me too plain. A travelling salesman took the photograph on an invention called a Brownie camera. He tried to convince me to buy one, but it cost a small fortune and I decided I would be better spending the money on my passage home and marrying Chrissie. Although it might be a wrench for her to leave her home, I am sure Chrissie will love Canada as much as I do once she becomes used to the vast open landscapes that are so different from our own small island.

I have booked passage and am due to arrive in Glasgow by mid-April, so will arrive in Lochmaddy as soon after that as possible. My mother and father will put me up until we leave for Canada. Please be good enough to speak to the Minister and make all the arrangements. I shall recompense you for any outlays you incur. As I need to be back in Canada as soon as possible, I have booked passage for Chrissie and me on the Scotian to return to Canada on 2nd May.

Yours truly

Your friend Roderick

I felt my blood rising again at the thought that my father had been discussing this matter with Roderick's family but not with me then sighed as I realised there was no point in complaining. I had been promised to this man and that was it as far as my family were concerned. I looked at the grainy photograph. I had only seen photographs in the newspapers, never the real thing so was impressed that this man had a photograph to send me. It was difficult to tell if Roderick was 'too plain', but he appeared to be tall and muscular plus he had a house and a farm, so he wasn't too poor either.

Perhaps getting married to this Roderick wasn't such a bad idea after all. He had property that he owned, and there was plenty of land to go round in Canada, so no one would come to make us homeless. I wouldn't need to get my sister up and do all the chores that Mother and Father expected of me as well as work at the big house. I looked at the letter again and realised that I had four months of freedom before he would arrive. If Roderick had his way, we would be married and off to Canada by the beginning of May. My heart was beating fast at the thought of being married. As his wife, I would need to become one flesh with Roderick, although I wasn't quite sure what that meant, only that a baby was usually the result. A baby was the last thing I wanted as I had heard Mother's screams when my brothers and sister were born, and it sounded too painful. I sighed and went through to face Father and Mother again.

Morag was sitting at the table with a bowl of broth in front of her and looked up when I came through. She didn't say anything at the sight of my tear-stained face, and I assumed Mother must have warned her not to.

'Come and sit down, Chrissie,' said Mother, placing another bowl of broth on the table. 'We've been telling Morag your news.'

'Thank you, *Mathair*. I'm sorry *Athair* for making such a fuss.'

'It won't be so bad, Chrissie. You'll see. Roderick comes from a good family. I will get a message to Reverend McEwan, and we can set a date for the marriage.'

From that day onwards, I looked at the grainy picture he had sent with his letter, wondering whether he was the man I wanted to marry. I hadn't seen Colin since that day in January, as he had gone back to Sandhurst where his father had insisted he go after leaving university. I foolishly wondered whether he would be

16

disappointed when he found out that I was now betrothed to someone else. There would be no more putting his arms around me and asking for kisses now. I realised I felt something like regret for my lost opportunity to become Master Colin's wife.

The wedding was set for the first of May, but Roderick had not arrived by mid-April. I wondered if he had been lost at sea. It still happened, even though the old sailing ships had been replaced by the new steamships which made the journey from Scotland to the other side of the world in less than two weeks now. Perhaps the fierceness of the ocean would save me from this terrible fate. I bit my lip and asked God to forgive me for having such a thought. I didn't wish Roderick any ill.

Mother was becoming increasingly fraught as the time drew closer to the date set for my marriage, but tried not to show it.

'Only a week to go, Chrissie, and you'll meet your betrothed. Aren't you excited?' she said one morning.

'Not particularly. What if he doesn't arrive in time or has changed his mind? It will be such an embarrassment if we need to cancel the wedding.'

She looked doubtful for a minute, but then painted on her smile again.

'Don't be so pessimistic, Chrissie. Look, the market is on in Lochmaddy this Saturday. Let's all go along and see if we can pick up some things for the wedding. Your marriage is something to celebrate.'

The market at Lochmaddy was a highlight of island life, and I couldn't help the rush of excitement I felt at the thought of going along. If I had known what was going to happen, I wouldn't have been so enthusiastic about it.

17

CHAPTER FOUR

Saturday dawned bright and clear and there was an air of excitement in the MacIntosh household. Everyone woke up early and got up without Mother having to call us, even Morag. We all mucked in and completed the chores in double quick time. I wore a light blue dress with tiny yellow flowers on it, my Sunday boots, and a yellow bonnet that I kept especially for sunny days. It was as good as when Victoria had given it to me last year as the island didn't have an abundance of sunny days. But today would be different, I thought, as we all climbed into the cart that would take us to Lochmaddy. Fluffy clouds were floating serenely across the sky, not scudding across the way they usually did. My heart was aflutter with excitement, and I recognised it wasn't just because of the market.

As we approached Lochmaddy, we joined a throng of other islanders going in the same direction. There was an air of excitement and lots of chatter and greetings between the various family groups moving in the same direction. I spotted Janet and asked Mother if I could walk with her for the last part of the journey.

'Yes, of course, but don't get lost. Remember, we're here with a purpose.'

'Yes, *Mathair*. How could I forget?' I said, jumping down from the cart and swinging my hips with what I hoped was a hint of defiance. Although I had accepted that it was my duty to marry this Roderick, I wasn't happy about it and wanted to let Mother know.

I quickly caught up with Janet and slipped my arm through hers.

'Hello, betrothed one,' said Janet, smiling a welcome at me.

I frowned theatrically, then smiled back at my friend. I thought about how I had needed to break the news of my impending marriage to Janet, Mrs McAllister, and Victoria after receiving the news of the arrival of my bridegroom. Mrs McAllister was very unhappy.

'You can't leave us in the lurch like that, Chrissie.'

18

'I know and I'm sorry, Mrs McAllister, but it's all happened so quickly, and he's booked the passage back so I can't really delay the wedding and my departure.'

'Well, it's a fine turn of events, is all I can say. Poor Miss Victoria will be lost without you. You are a selfish girl.'

These remarks hurt me. How could I be selfish? It was not what I wanted. I didn't want to marry a stranger who was old enough to be my father. Tears stung my eyes, and I rubbed them with the back of my hand as I left the housekeeper and made my way up to Miss Victoria to tell her the news. How grateful I was when Miss Victoria had a different reaction.

'Oh, Chrissie! How romantic and exciting. To have someone come all the way over from Canada to marry you and take you to a new life. I wish my father had promised me to someone when I was little before these legs stopped working.'

I could feel the tears beginning again, but for Miss Victoria this time. My heart was sore at the thought of the little Victoria being able to run and skip like everyone else and then the use of her legs being stolen from her by the polio together with the chance of marrying anyone too. I hugged her warmly and told her how much I would miss her, while she promised to write to me every month and send me the magazines that we both loved so much.

The clip clop of a horse and the sound of a man's voice telling the crowd to move out of the way brought me back to the present. As Janet and I pulled each other into the side of the path, I looked up to see who this ignorant man was. My heart missed a beat when I saw it was Master Colin, looking all high and mighty on a black mare.

'Good morning Chrissie,' he said, taking off his hat and bowing theatrically towards me.

'Good morning Master Colin,' I replied, my face becoming warm when I remembered what had happened the last time we had met.

'What's wrong with you?' asked Janet. 'Your face is as red as the poppies that grow in the machair. It's only Master Colin.'

19

I then explained what had happened back in January and wondered why I hadn't told Janet before. I usually told her everything, but I remember being ashamed of the feelings he had awoken in me.

'No! he kissed you, how awful,' said Janet, in a voice that was too loud for my liking.

'Hush Janet. I don't want everyone to know,' I said, looking round the other people nearby to see if they had heard anything. I was glad to find that they were all too excited about going to the market to take any notice of two silly girls.

'What was it like?' whispered Janet. 'I haven't kissed a boy yet.'

'It was frightening but also exciting,' I said, realising that I was enjoying the retelling of this event. 'His lips were soft at first, but then he put his tongue into my mouth, and it was all wet.'

'No!'

'I think he wanted to,' I hesitated, trying to think of the right words, 'become one flesh with me and that was when I remembered the story you had told me about Sheona, and I ran away.'

'Oh Chrissie. You had a lucky escape. What would have happened if he had taken your virginity and then you had found out you were betrothed to this Roderick Macdonald?'

'It doesn't bear thinking about Janet. Let's change the subject, please. I am on my way to pick some ribbons and trinkets for my wedding dress. By the way, did I tell you that Miss Victoria is giving me a loan of a Shetland Marriage Shawl that she inherited from her grandmother? She says she's not likely to be needing it. It's so sad for her, isn't it?'

We continued on our way, chatting happily about my forthcoming wedding, at which Janet would be a witness. When we reached the Market Stance, I waved goodbye to her and made my way over to my family.

CHAPTER FIVE

Father, Johnny, and Lachlan headed towards the cattle and horses that were for sale, and no doubt Father and Johnny would have a dram in the whisky tent with the other men later. Lachlan was only sixteen so too young yet for alcohol. Luckily, my father and Johnny were happy drunks when they had a few drams, and I was glad that Mother and I didn't need to fear a change in temperament from the men in our family at the end of market day. Several other women were not so lucky and after the last market there had been loud shouting and swearing from some of the other black houses in our little community and mother and I had felt only sympathy when we saw a few of the women with their faces covered by their shawls the next day to conceal their bruises. I always prayed that the man I would marry would not be a drinker and luckily God at least answered this prayer.

Morag, despite being fourteen, wanted to go to the sweet stall and pulled excitedly on Mother's hand.

'Alright, alright, I'm coming,' she laughed, 'but after you make a choice of what you want, you need to come with Chrissie and me to the ribbon stall.'

'I will *Mathair*, I will.'

Merry children crowded around the sweet stall holding up half-pennies to buy from the array of brightly coloured sugary treats.

'I'll wait here until Morag gets her sweets, Chrissie. You go over and have a look at the other stalls to see if anything is to your liking. We'll catch you up.'

'Thanks, *Mathair*,' I said, relishing the thought of a wander on my own to browse the ribbons and trinkets.

I was peering at the spools of ribbon and lace when I felt the hairs on the back of my neck stand up. Putting my hand on my neck, I turned to see Master Colin looking down at me with a twinkle in his bright blue eyes.

'Hello Chrissie. It is lovely to see you here at the market. Look, Mr Chisholm is about to take a photograph. Shall we try to get

21

ourselves into it?' Colin said, grabbing my hand and pulling me towards where the Procurator Fiscal was setting up his tripod and camera to capture the locals at the market.

I knew I should not offer any encouragement to Master Colin, but he was not giving me much choice and I would really love to be in a photograph. So, holding on to my bonnet, I let him pull me into the crowd who were gathering to pose for the amateur photographer who was well known around the islands. After it was all over and people were dispersing, I withdrew my hand from Master Colin's and told him I would have to go back and meet my mother.

'You know I am to be married soon and I need to look for some ribbons and lace for my wedding dress.'

'Victoria told me your news, and I was so sad when I heard it. You are too beautiful to be married off to some old man from Canada,' he said, putting an arm around my waist and pulling me gently towards him.

I felt like his eyes were devouring me and my heart began to thump as his face moved closer to mine. Surely, he would not kiss me here in full view of everyone. He would shame me. I pushed him away, but he grabbed me and pressed his face close to mine. I could smell the whisky on his breath and felt a flutter of panic as he whispered words I did not like into my ear.

'Who do you think you are, Chrissie MacIntosh? You should consider yourself honoured that you have taken my fancy. Let's have no more of this pushing me away. My horse is over here. Let's ride off together and I'll break you in for your new husband.'

By now, he was gripping my wrist and pulling me towards his horse. No matter how hard I tried, I could not free myself from him. I caught sight of Mother in the distance and called out to her, but she was talking with a neighbour and didn't hear me. I cried and begged Colin to let me go. People were looking at us curiously, but no one intervened. Not until a tall man with a long coat and a wide-brimmed hat rode up on a buggy and jumped out.

'Are you alright, young lass?' he called.

22

'Keep out of this sir, the young lady is an employee in my father's household,' responded Colin before I could reply, but it was obvious to anyone with any sense that I was not alright.

'And what has she done that you need to hold her wrist so tightly? You are clearly hurting her. Let her go.'

Colin let my wrist go and went towards the man, all his anger now focussed on the stranger. He threw a punch, which the man avoided skilfully. The next thing I knew, the man had Colin in an armlock and was threatening him with the constable.

'Alright. You have her. She's not worth the trouble,' Colin sneered, as he picked up his hat and made his way over to his horse. The poor horse got the whip, and Colin and the mare sped off in a cloud of dust.

CHAPTER SIX

I could feel my legs giving way now that the danger was over, but luckily my rescuer caught me before I crumpled to the ground. He gazed at me intently and I noticed his eyes were bright blue, just like Colin's. That made me feel anxious, and I hoped I hadn't fallen from the frying pan into the fire. He was tall and muscular and wore a bushy auburn moustache. There was something familiar about him, but I couldn't put my finger on what it was. Perhaps it was just that his eyes were so like Colin's. By this time, a small crowd had gathered round us, curious to find out what had happened. I spotted Mrs Campbell, a neighbour who liked to gossip, which made me aware that I was being held in the powerful arms of a man I didn't know and thought it best to move. No point in giving her anything more to gossip about.

'Thank you, sir. You may let me go now.'

'If you're sure. You seem a little shaken. Can I take you to your family perhaps if they are here?'

'Thank you, sir, my *Mathair* is over there at the ribbon and jewellery stall.'

He gently took my arm and escorted me towards where Mother and Morag were. Turning round, Mother smiled as she spotted us, but her smile faded when she saw the distress that I was in.

'What's happened, Chrissie? Come here *mo ghraidh*,'

I willingly went into her arms, where all my fear and anguish poured out in heartrending sobs.

'Oh *Mathair*. It was Master Colin. He was trying to get me to go with him and I think he wanted to... to hurt me.'

Mother's face darkened.

'Morag run and get your *Athair*. He's gone too far this time.'

'If it wasn't for this man, I don't know what would have happened.'

Mother turned her attention to the stranger now, and I saw a look of recognition crossing her face and I knew then why he looked familiar.

24

'Roderick? Is it you?'

'It is me, Marion. All the way from Canada.'

'I don't know whether to laugh or cry. This is such a terrible thing that has happened to Chrissie, but it is a wonderful thing that you have made it home safe. Come here.'

Her slight frame wrapped him in her arms as best she could, laughing and crying at the same time.

'What the hell's going on here?' Father called, taking in the state I was in and the hugging that was going on between his wife and a strange man.

Roderick turned away from Mother and before Father knew what had happened, Roderick enveloped him in his arms too.

'Angus, Angus, it is your old friend Roderick come all the way from Canada,' said Mother, going over and hugging the two of them now.

After the hugging and the clapping on the back was finished, Father turned to me. By this time, I was no longer sobbing but was feeling the worse for wear and had the beginning of a large bruise on my wrist. At Father's look of concern, I sobbed quietly again, and let Mother explain what had happened with Master Colin. This only made me feel worse though when I heard the word molest being used.

'That ruffian. I shall have him charged with assault. Do not worry, *mo ghraidh*. He won't get away with it.'

If Father meant to go to the constable I would be shamed. He would be bound to take Master Colin's side and say I was to blame, that I had encouraged Master Colin by posing for the photograph with him. Maybe Roderick wouldn't want to marry me if he thought I had been flirting with Master Colin. What would happen then? Luckily my mother saved the day.

'Don't be blethering, man,' said Mother. 'The constable won't take any action against him. He's the Laird's nephew. Better that you go see Master Colin's father and tell him what's happened. Leave it up to him to deal with his son.'

'I still have a week's notice to work *Mathair*, but I don't want to go back.'

'Don't you worry, Chrissie. You won't be setting foot over that door again. Your *Athair* will collect your wages when he goes to see the Factor.'

'But Miss Victoria was going to lend me her grandmother's shawl for the wedding,' I said, looking shyly over at Roderick.

'You'll take nothing from that family,' answered Father. 'Your *Mathair* will make you whatever you need. Let's get you home. An early night is what you need.'

CHAPTER SEVEN

I woke up like every other day I could remember to the sound of Mother calling me and the familiar smells of peat smoke, oatmeal cooking on the fire and the stink of animals, but today the smell of cooking chickens, lambs, oatcakes, and sweet cake blended with these familiar smells. The reason was that today was my wedding day. The house had been a hive of activity for the past week, with all the women helping Mother pluck chickens and the men slaughtering lambs to prepare for this big day. Since the Saturday Market, I had seen Roderick several times but always in the company of my mother and father or his mother and father, so I still didn't know him all that well. However, I got the sense that he was a good man and would look after me just the way he had done when Colin had tried to take me away.

I didn't return to the Factor's house, but Victoria had sent me a lovely letter together with her grandmother's shawl, wishing me well and hoping that I had recovered from the scare her stupid brother had caused me. She also told me that when her father had given Colin a telling off, he had turned on him and told him he was leaving Sandhurst as he didn't want to be a soldier. There had been a terrible row and Colin had left home and she didn't know where he was now. Her father had deliberately sent him to the Military Academy when he finished at university to see if it would teach him some self-discipline and make a better man of him, but unfortunately, it didn't look as if it had worked. I felt relieved that I wouldn't need to see him again.

For once, Morag was awake and didn't need to be coaxed into getting up. The entire family was excited about the wedding, probably if truth be told more so than I was. My sister was especially excited as Mother had made a new dress for her and bought new boots for her to wear with it. Normally she ran about barefoot, except for Sundays. She was now almost fourteen and was taking an interest in clothes. It wouldn't be long until she would be leaving school and trying to find work. In other circumstances,

I would have suggested that she could replace me as Miss Victoria's companion, but after what happened with Colin, Father would never agree to it. I was about to get up when Mother walked through the curtain carrying a cup of tea.

'Good morning Chrissie, this is for you.'

'For me *Mathair*, but you never bring me tea in bed.'

'Well, it is a special day and I want to have a wee chat with you.'

My heart sank. I hoped Mother was not going to talk to me about personal things. I could feel my cheeks growing pink at the thought.

'Morag, your porridge is waiting for you. Go on through to the table.'

'But I want to hear what you're going to say to Chrissie.'

'Sorry, this is a grown-up conversation. I will talk to you in the same way on your wedding day. Run along, there's a good girl.'

'So *mo ghraidh*, how are you feeling?' she said, turning her attention to me and handing over the cup of hot, sweet tea.

'I'm feeling fine, *Mathair*,' I sighed.

'You don't sigh like that if you're feeling fine.'

'Well, I suppose I am a wee bit nervous. Everything has happened so fast, and I feel like I'm marrying a stranger. I'm also worried about what will happen after the wedding ceremony.'

Mother smiled and folded my hand in hers.

'There's no need to worry about that yet. You will sleep here tonight, and Roderick will sleep at his parents' house. Canada will be where you will come together as husband and wife. But tell me what's troubling you.'

'Well, Colin scared me, the way he was so forceful. Do you think Roderick will be like that?' I asked, moving into a topic of conversation I thought I didn't want to have with my mother.

'Well, I think Roderick will be considerate, but it is always difficult for women the first time and can be painful. You have seen how the animals breed, so you know what it will be like for you and

28

Roderick. We women just need to put up with it. But if we are lucky, we can enjoy the physical side of marriage too.'

I was horrified as the image of the rams mounting the ewes on the croft came into my mind, but I didn't say that to Mother. That was a step too far in this discussion.

'And you understand that when you and Roderick do become intimate, you will more than likely have a baby?.'

'Oh *Mathair,* I'm terrified at the thought of having a baby. I heard your screams when the midwife was delivering Morag and Lachlan.'

'I know how you feel. I felt like that when I was your age, but you'll get over the pain when you have your own *leanabh* lying in your arms,' Mother said, rubbing my arm. 'Roderick will no doubt want children to help him run the farm and to pass it on to, so you will just need to do your duty. '

Mother paused, and I wondered what embarrassing topic of conversation she was going to have with me now.

'There are ways that women can stop themselves from having a baby, but I don't know what they are. Maybe you could find a book to tell you about it.'

I was shocked. I had never heard even a whisper that girls could stop themselves having a baby and here was my mother telling me to find a book about it. Where would I find such a book?

'Come on. Let's get you up and dressed.'

CHAPTER EIGHT

When I was ready to go, I went through the curtain where Father was waiting for me. As he gazed at me, his normally stern face softened.

'You are beautiful, *mo ghraidh*. Where has my little girl gone?'

'I'm still here inside *Dadaidh*,' I said, pointing at my heart. 'I will always be your little girl.'

He hugged me close, and my eyes misted up as I realised how much I would miss that mix of pipe smoke and animal that was my father's special smell. I knew that as my father, he was prejudiced, but I must admit, I felt beautiful. I just wished I could feel happier, but I still had some misgivings about this marriage that they had forced me into. Mother had made me a new navy-blue dress and the Shetland Lace Shawl that Victoria had sent over for me complemented it. Morag had picked some wildflowers from the machair, and Mother had tied them with a navy-blue ribbon we had bought at the market. I didn't exactly feel like a princess but couldn't help hoping that I had met my prince.

The Reverend McEwan performed the ceremony after our wedding party had walked round the church, as was the tradition, and I couldn't help shedding a tear when Roderick and I made our vows to one another.

'*Tha mise,* Roderick Macdonald,' he began reciting the traditional Gaelic wedding vow, and looking into my eyes he promised to love, honour, and cherish me in sickness and in health till God would separate us by death. I happily repeated the vow, never thinking how much these words would test me in the future. Afterwards, everyone went back to the school hall where there were speeches, lots of food and drink followed by a ceilidh. It felt like everyone on the island was there; the schoolroom was so packed. Because it was a beautiful night, people spilled outside into the school garden. I became caught up in the music of the fiddles and the accordions and danced like there was no tomorrow with Roderick, who swept me round the floor in his powerful arms,

30

whirling and hooching with exuberance. I was glad to see that he didn't take any of the whisky, port or beer that was on offer to the men. Not like my brother, Johnny, who was staggering around when he was jigging, leaving his poor partner to hold him upright. I was especially pleased when Mr Chisholm came and took a photograph of the wedding party for his records, promising to send a copy to us when he had developed it. Finally, it was all over, and the fiddler played a slow lament to send us on our way home.

As Roderick and I made our way hand in hand back to my parents' house under the vast dark sky full of twinkling stars, how I wished we could be together tonight and get the whole thing over with. But it couldn't be. There was no room in either of our family homes for us to sleep together. But I guessed he would want to kiss me now that we were married. Butterflies danced a ceilidh of their own in my stomach as thoughts of what it would be like, pecked at my head like hens in a coup. What if he was rough like Colin when he kissed me? What if I didn't like the way he kissed? That wet tongue of Colin's had put me off kissing. As if he sensed my nervousness, Roderick stopped, turned me towards him, and took both my hands. This is it, I thought as he enfolded them in his own.

'Thank you for marrying me, Chrissie. I will do my best to be a good husband to you.'

Taking my face in his hands, he kissed me lightly on the lips. His kiss was sweet and tender, nothing like Colin's. My knees became weak with relief, and he had to steady me in his arms. But he did not kiss me again. It surprised me at how disappointed I felt.

'Let's get you home, Chrissie. We have a long journey ahead of us tomorrow.'

CHAPTER NINE

The next couple of days passed in a daze for me. I had never been off the island before, so everything was new to my eye. I was sick going over the Minch, but luckily my mother had packed a damp cloth and towel for me in case I needed it. Passengers were sick all the time, as the Minch was well known for its rough waters. I prayed that the trip across the Atlantic would be less difficult, but I didn't hold out much hope. Roderick was quiet for most of the journey on the train down to Glasgow. He seemed a man of few words and sat staring out of the window for most of the journey. I wondered what he was thinking about, but I was so enthralled by the beautiful scenery that I wasn't too bothered. I had never seen such tall mountains, lush woodlands, or so many villages with houses that were not black houses.

When we arrived at Glasgow Central Station, Aunt Katie was waiting for us. Although Roderick had been reluctant, we were to spend the night with her as our ship wasn't leaving the Broomielaw until the following morning. If we hadn't stayed at Katie's house, we would have needed to hang about the port until the morning. The house where she stayed was in a place called Plantation, which made me think of slaves. I was sure that slaves used to work on plantations to grow cotton, but I couldn't be certain. The station was buzzing with noise, not only from the loud whistles and puff puffs of the steam trains, but from the number of people making their way on and off the platforms. I had never seen so many people and could hardly contain my excitement. This was going to be an adventure.

'Chrissie, Chrissie come here, my darling. It is so lovely to see you. How long is it? Let me look at you. My oh my, you are quite the lady now. The last time I saw you, you were in pigtails and your school pinafore.'

'Hello Aunt Katie,' I said, loving the hint of perfume I could smell from her as I cuddled her. I must ask what it is. Perhaps I could get some now that I was a married woman. I suddenly remembered Roderick and turned towards him.

'And this is my husband, Roderick, Aunt Katie.'

'Hello Roddy.'

'Hello Katie.'

There was a brief pause before they shook hands. I sensed a tension between them and wondered why. I thought it strange that my aunt had used the more intimate form of Roderick.

'So, you two know each other, then?'

'We do, Chrissie, we do,' said Roderick, but he didn't go on to give me any explanation.

Neither did Katie.

'Right, well, let's get you over to my house. I've hired a horse and buggy with a driver, so we'll be there in no time,' she said, ushering us out of the station.

It took us about half an hour to reach Katie's house, but what an exciting trip it was. Although Glasgow was dirty and noisy in comparison with North Uist, my aunt pointed out landmarks along the way. I had never seen so many tall buildings and wondered what it must be like to live on top of one another. The grandest building we passed had a golden angel that sat upon its roof and housed a large emporium on the ground floor. She also pointed out slightly further along a beautiful sandstone building, which she told me was a library where anyone could select books to read. I briefly wondered if I might get the type of book my mother had suggested about how to stop a baby being made.

'Andrew Carnegie donated it,' my aunt told me. I looked at her blankly and she continued, 'You know the Scottish/American Philanthropist.'

I had never heard of him, but didn't want to show my ignorance, so said nothing.

'This is it,' said Aunt Katie, smiling proudly when the cab pulled up outside a red sandstone tenement like all the other ones that had lined the streets we had passed through. 'I live on the first floor and have two rooms. I share a water closet on the landing with my two neighbours and we all take turns to keep it clean.'

I was thrilled to think that there was a real flushing water closet.

'Oh, this is beautiful, Aunt Katie. I've never seen anything so grand and look at the lights,' I said as we entered a close with green shiny tiles halfway up the walls bordered with a green and yellow floral pattern and a lamp on the walls.

'Yes, they're powered by gas. I have gas lights in my house too, although at this time of year we don't need them.'

The driver helped us carry our travel chest up the stairs, and Roderick handed him some coppers for his trouble. Inside the house was a small hall with two doors leading off. Aunt Katie showed us round explaining that one room was a kitchen/living area, and the other room was her bedroom. I wondered where Roderick and I would sleep as there appeared to be only one bed and, as if she had read my mind, Katie explained the sleeping arrangements.

'So, I've put fresh sheets on my bed for you and Roddy,' she said, and I thought her cheeks grew rather pink as she looked at us. 'You will start on a long journey tomorrow on board that ship, and I dare say it will be none too comfortable. So, I thought you would enjoy a soft cosy bed for one night at least.'

'That is very kind of you, Katie,' said Roderick. 'but where will you sleep?'

'Look,' she said, pulling back a curtain in the kitchen/living area with a flourish. 'I have another bed in here, in the recess. I'm very lucky to have this extra space. My neighbours on either side have four children each and I don't know how they fit them all into two rooms.'

I couldn't concentrate on what my aunt was saying as I was thinking about sharing a bed with Roderick and it was making my stomach flutter wildly.

CHAPTER TEN

I needn't have worried, as Roderick merely pecked me on the cheek, said goodnight and turned away from me. He was sleeping soundly within minutes. I lay awake for a long time, undecided whether to feel relieved or disappointed. After Katie had made us supper, despite me prattling on about our journey from North Uist, we had sat in an uncomfortable silence at times with only the ticking of the wall clock to break the hush. There was something between Katie and Roderick that I didn't understand, and I was curious about what it was, but thought it best not to ask. I decided I would wait until we were on board ship before bringing up the subject with Roderick.

We awoke and rose before sunrise, both making our preparations for departure in silence. I felt less close to Roderick than I had before we arrived in Glasgow. Katie bustled about preparing porridge, tea, and toast for us, but I didn't feel much like eating and left most of it on the plate to congeal and grow cold. There was a sharp knock at the door which announced the arrival of the driver who would take us to the Broomielaw, where our ship would leave for Montreal. When I went to kiss Aunt Katie goodbye, I clung to her like a limpet, suddenly not wanting to leave her or Scotland. It was she who needed to take my arms from her and push me away, tears streaming down both our cheeks.

By the time we arrived at the Broomielaw, the sun had come up. Despite the time of year, it was a wintery, watery sun that promised rough waters on our journey to Montreal. The lacklustre sun was easily dulled by the grey and black smoke spewing out from the huge chimney sitting above the cabins for those travelling first and second class on the Scotian, the ship that would take us to a new life. Clustered around the chimney hung several lifeboats. I shivered and prayed to God that we wouldn't need to use them. As I looked at the other travellers who stood in untidy groups, I sensed an air of hushed excitement and dread hovering over us, but perhaps it was just me. The sombre dark greys, blues, and

35

browns we were clad in for the journey reflected our dark mood. We stamped our boots on the cobbled quayside, trying to keep warm and to quell the mounting restlessness to get going, to get on with this journey into the unknown.

I had never felt so alone as I thought again about last night. I had hoped that Roderick might have tried to become intimate with me, but when he had turned away, the fluttering butterflies in my stomach had turned into a hard knot of dread. What if he found me unattractive? What if he didn't love me? Suddenly, my thoughts and the hush were shattered, as the port became alive with sounds. There was the boom, boom of the pistons as they turned over, preparing for the journey ahead and the piercing sound of the horn warning us to get ready for boarding. The clatter of heavy carts being wheeled by stevedores towards the ship carrying our possessions in their rickety care added to the noise and I wondered if we would be safely reunited with them when we reached our destination. There were horses pulling carts with cargo for the ship, dropping their manure everywhere as they clip clopped along the cobbled quay. The reek mingled with the smell of the coal and the steam and my fear.

The first week of our journey was as bad as I had suspected it might be. My heart sank when the crew directed us and a thousand other passengers to the bowels of the ship for our accommodation in steerage class. It was a barbaric method of travel. The ship's crew separated us into three groups: married couples and children in one area, single men in another, and single women in another. They gave us bunks to sleep in, which had very little privacy, with only a mean curtain separating us from the other passengers. Food was disgusting and the kitchen crew ladled it out to us as if we were the occupants of a poorhouse instead of pioneers making our way to a new life to help a new country.

But worse than our sleeping quarters was the Atlantic weather, and I feared at one point that we would need to use the lifeboats I had spotted before we set off. The first night was calm, but for the following five days, the rain pounded the ship in heavy bursts of

36

water that ricocheted off the deck like bullets from a gun and the screaming wind battered our bodies and tore at our clothes like banshees whenever we ventured up on deck to escape the cramped, foul hold of the Scotian. I had been sick crossing over the Minch, but it was nothing to the sickness that I and hundreds of other passengers experienced in that pitching ship ploughing its way through huge waves, the likes of which I had never seen before despite the frequent storms we experienced back home. We worried that typhoid might make its way through the ship as the sanitary conditions were so bad, which would mean the authorities would quarantine the ship when we got to Montreal. I think I dreaded the thought of spending a minute longer on that ship than I needed more than I dreaded catching the typhoid.

But worse than these conditions was what I found out about Roderick and Katie. It was about mid-way through the journey when we had gone up on deck for some fresh air. There was a sense amongst us passengers that the worst was over, and we were closer to our destination than our departure point. As we looked out at the endless ocean, deceptively calm and beautiful now that the earlier storms had passed, I took Roderick's hand. I wanted to draw him closer to me. Someone was playing a harmonica and other couples on deck were dancing slowly together.

'It's beautiful Roderick isn't it? Shall we have a dance like the other couples? I long to feel your arms around me.'

I looked at him expectantly, putting my face upwards, hoping that he would take me in his arms and lower his lips to mine, but it was not to be.

'There's something I need to let you know, Chrissie. It's playing on my mind, and until I tell you I don't feel it would be appropriate for me to kiss you.'

I knew it. He didn't love me. But if he didn't love me, why had he come all the way to Scotland to marry me. It made little sense. My heart was beating fast in my breast and my breath was coming out in short bursts.

'Let's sit down over here, Chrissie,' he said, leading me towards a wooden bench. 'Have you ever wondered why your father promised your hand to me when you were so young?'

'Yes, of course. I didn't think it was right to do that. What if you had met someone else, or I had met someone else? You were away for a long time Roderick.'

'I know. So why do you think he did it?'

'Well, he said that you had been there on the day I was born and had always taken an interest in me after that. I remember you used to brush my hair when I was little and that I asked you to marry me. You didn't agree to marry me because of that, did you?'

'No,' he said, smiling. 'The truth is, your Aunt Katie and I were promised to one another, and that was why I used to be at your croft all the time.'

'Aunt Katie!'

I was stunned. None of my family had ever mentioned it. But if they were betrothed, why had they not married?

'So that's why she called you Roddy and there was an awkwardness between you.'

'You noticed that then. I wasn't sure if you had. But it's been playing on my mind, and I thought you might ask me about her.'

'Why didn't you marry her? I don't understand.'

'It's a long story, but basically she jilted me. Your father had given me money to buy the tickets for us to go to Canada, but after I had bought them and they had arranged the wedding, she took cold feet and ran away to Glasgow.'

'Ran away. How awful for you. You must have felt humiliated.'

'I was, but so was your father. She had brought shame to your family by running away like that and I think he was trying to make me feel better by offering me your hand in marriage when you grew up.'

'So, you never loved me. I was a substitute for Katie.'

'How could I love a five-year-old Chrissie? It would have been odd, don't you think? I only agreed to become betrothed to you for

38

your father's sake. He was so distressed, and I wanted him to feel better.'

'But what made you come back now? It's been fifteen years.'

'I received a letter from my father. He told me you had grown into a pretty, young woman, and he wondered whether I had any plans to keep Angus MacIntosh to his promise of your hand in marriage. Your father had confided in him that he had heard rumours the Factor's son, Colin, was trying to turn your head and he was worried that you would end up shamed.'

My face burned. How on earth had my father found out about Master Colin? It must have been Mrs McAllister who was friendly with my mother. She must have seen him flirting with me whenever he was home. No wonder *Athair* was so angry and wanted to call the constable after what happened at the market.

'So, your father and mine conspired together to save me from Colin. But that doesn't explain why you came. You owed me nothing.'

'I must confess that I was not being noble. Until recently, I had a housekeeper who had been with me for many years. Sadly, she died, and I needed either another housekeeper or a wife. Women are indispensable to the running of the farms in the Canadian prairies, but they are hard to find. Some men resort to mail order brides.'

'But you didn't need to order one by mail. You had me, who was being handed over to you on a platter like a slab of fish.'

'I'm sorry Chrissie. I know it sounds like you are just part of some business deal, but I am sure we will grow to love each other in time.'

I was heartbroken. Although I had been reluctant to marry Roderick and was doing it from duty, I had also hoped for love. I thought he had come for me because he had always been in love with me. What a joke. I was going to be twenty in June, but my life felt like it was already over.

CHAPTER ELEVEN

I was dazed and nauseous when we arrived in Montreal but luckily I hadn't caught typhoid and neither had any of the other passengers, so our ship wasn't quarantined. I could hardly believe it was only a couple of weeks since Roderick and I had married and began our journey to Canada. It felt like a couple of months. And our journey wasn't over. We had barely time to draw breath at Montreal before we were sitting on the locomotive that would take us on our two-day journey to Saskatchewan. At least the train was a little more comfortable than the ship, but I felt out of place among the mostly male travellers, rough working men who were making their way west to work for the railroad or on the prairie farms and Indian men who sat looking at me with inscrutable eyes. I had known that Canada was much bigger than Scotland, but I had never realised how large or how varied the landscape was. We moved through lush green countryside, built up towns and vast tracts of barren wasteland that was totally uninhabited. Hotels along the way provided our meals, which gave some respite from the carriage we sat in, making half-hearted conversation with each other and some of the other passengers.

When eventually we arrived in Saltcoats, the town that was nearest to Roderick's homestead, we stopped outside the Golden Sheaf Hotel, a two-storey timber building with balconies wrapped around the first floor.

'Let's go in here for lunch while we wait for Frankie to pick us up.'

'But I thought women weren't allowed in bars, Roderick? I don't want to go into a place that people would think was improper.'

'It's alright. Bill Preston and his wife are part of the temperance movement, and they turned the hotel into an alcohol-free place when they bought it a few years ago. His wife Jeannie is a member of the Homemakers' Club, and she has set it up so that the farming women in these parts can have somewhere to rest when they come into town.'

40

'Hello Roddy. It is good to see you back. Is this your new wife then?' said a man, about the same age as Roderick, when we entered the hotel. He was handsome, but thinner than Roderick. Obviously, running a bar was less physically demanding than running a farm. He had short brown hair, brown eyes, and I noticed his teeth were rather brown, too. He was sucking on a large cigar.

'Yes, this is Chrissie,' Roderick smiled, putting his arm around my waist, and drawing me in to him proprietorially. It was the first time he had held me close, and I could feel the warmth of his firm body through my dress. My head spun slightly as I put my hand out to greet the barman.

'I'm pleased to meet you, Chrissie. I am Bill Preston, the owner of this modest establishment. Welcome to Canada.'

'Thank you, Mr Preston. I am happy to be here. Hopefully, I shall settle as the journey from Scotland was a difficult one and I wouldn't like to make it again.'

'I'll just call my wife, Jeannie. She's been looking forward to meeting you.'

'Did I hear someone call my name?' said a woman with bright red hair and freckles who appeared at the back of Bill.

'Hello sweetheart,' he said. 'This is Chrissie, Roddy's new wife.'

'How do Chrissie?' she said, holding out her hand to shake mine. The woman was older than me, but she had a friendly air and I felt comforted that I would have someone to talk to about women's interests. As we all chatted together while waiting for our lunch to be served, Bill suddenly remembered something that had happened while Roderick was in Scotland.

'You won't have heard Roderick, but while you were away, the old Adam's place was sold to another homesteader, and you'll never guess what he found when he started tilling the soil?'

Roderick said nothing, but Bill continued as if he had asked him what the man had found.

'A skeleton. It was old, but he could tell that the man had been shot right through the middle.'

'A skeleton,' I said, my stomach clenching with a mix of fear and excitement. 'But how did it get there and who was he?'

'Well, it looks like it might be the previous owner of the homestead, Jim Adams. He went missing not long before we bought the hotel from Harold Winter. Did you know either of them, Roderick?'

'Well, I knew Harold, of course, but no, I don't think I ever met Jim Adams.'

'There was a missing person poster outside the post office when Jeannie and I moved in. When I asked about it, I was told that this Jim Adams had gone missing the previous winter. People had seen him go into the hotel with his wife, a Cree squaw, but no one had seen them come out. His horse and buggy were missing, and he was never found, nor was the squaw.'

'Yes, I vaguely remember something about that. This place was wild in those days with lonely angry men and too much drink, creating a fever in them.'

'Apparently the land lay empty for all those years as the authorities were first of all trying to trace Adams and his wife. When they failed at that they began trying to trace relatives and apparently they found someone in England all these years later who told them to put it up for sale. Aleksander Bukowski bought it as it was on the boundary of his land.'

'Have the Mounted Police been told about the skeleton?' asked Roderick.

'Yeh. Aleksander got the fright of his life when he discovered it and was on the phone to them straight away. He sure was shook up when he called into the hotel last month and did a lot of complaining about not being able to get a whisky.'

'Will he be able to continue to get the land tilled or will he need to wait until the Mounties get round to solving the mystery?'

'No, they've removed the skeleton and have told him he can keep going with the ploughing. They said it looks like it happened over ten years ago, so they don't intend to do much investigating.

They've just put up a poster asking if anyone knows anything to contact them.'

I didn't know what to think. How dreadful for that man finding a skeleton on his land. I hoped the place wasn't as rowdy and lawless as it had obviously been back then.

CHAPTER TWELVE

Roderick didn't speak of the skeleton to me, nor did he eat much of the roast beef and potatoes that Jeannie gave us for lunch. He had made more of an effort on the ship to make conversation with me after his revelation about him and Katie, but he seemed to be back inside his head again. When we had finished, we picked up our supplies for the week and set off in the horse and buggy that Roderick's farm hand Frankie had driven in to pick us up. Frankie was a young man, not much older than me, with brown hair and mischievous green eyes. His face lit up when he saw Roderick, but he looked down shyly when Roderick introduced him to me.

'Pleased to meet you, Ma'am,' he said, taking his hat off. 'It will take us about an hour to drive to the homestead. Mrs Bukowski and Heather are waiting for you, boss.'

I assumed the women must be neighbours, waiting to welcome us, and I looked forward to meeting these people who would soon become part of my life. The journey took slightly more than an hour and it was an uncomfortable ride bumping up and down over the rough path. When we stopped to open a gate, Roderick explained that this was his homestead. We drove through fields and fields of what I assumed was corn, its green shoots just poking through the red earth.

'It's a mix of oats and wheat, Chrissie. We rotate the fields so that the crops grow better.'

'And did you plough all this land yourself Roderick when you first arrived?'

'Not all of it, but most of it. I loved every moment of those early days,' he said with a dreamy look in his eyes. 'It was hard work, but it was good for my soul. There is no other feeling like it when it's just you and the plough moving over that virgin soil that has lain untouched since God created the earth.'

I felt goosebumps as Roderick described this experience. He had been so quiet most of the time since I had met him, it surprised me at how expressively he described his experience to me.

44

At length Roderick pointed out a house in the distance, which he said was to be my new home. As we drew closer, I was relieved to see that it wasn't a black house and there were separate quarters for the animals. It was a two-storey house built of timber, with several windows set into the walls and tiles on the roof. A wooden porch surrounded the house with a couple of rocking chairs, which looked a very welcoming place to sit of a summer evening. As well as the house, there was a yard where chickens were clucking about in a coop, a barn, a fenced-in field where several horses were grazing, and a shieling fashioned from old bits of wood and metal. There was also what looked like a well-tended vegetable garden.

'Welcome to your new home, Chrissie,' Roderick said, when we had dismounted from the buggy. 'It's a traditional homestead cabin. A specialist company produces them in kit form and then delivers them to us homesteaders by horse and cart. It has a basement and an upper floor where the bedrooms are. The house is cool in summer and warm in winter, which is just perfect for the extremes of weather we get here in Canada.'

'It looks nicer than the black houses that we're used to, Roderick. I cannot wait for you to take me round the farm. Everything is so spacious here,' I said, scanning over the seemingly endless fields of green shoots that surrounded us. 'It's so different from our small island. But tell me, what is that little shieling used for?'

'That was the shanty I lived in when I came out here at first, but now Frankie, Hamish and Jake, who help around the farm, live there.'

'Live there? It doesn't look habitable.'

'I can assure you it is quite comfortable and is standard accommodation for the hands in these parts. Come on, there's someone who can't wait to meet you.' he said, reaching for my hand and drawing me towards the house.

Despite knowing that ours was a business arrangement rather than a love match, I still felt a pang of disappointment when he didn't scoop me up in his arms and carry me over the threshold in traditional newlywed style. But what else could I expect. He seemed impervious to me. He had shown more emotion when talking about tilling the land than he had towards me. I wondered if he would even sleep with me tonight and consummate our marriage, or would he do what he had done in Glasgow and turn away from me.

When we went inside, the door opened straight into a large room which was furnished with a rough wooden table with eight chairs pushed under it, a writing bureau, a shelf with books and a proper fireplace with a couple of armchairs that looked well-worn set at either side of the fireplace. I noticed there was a newer chair that looked as if it had yet to be sat in and wondered if Roderick had got it especially for me. There was a stove in the corner, with a kettle bubbling in welcome.

Standing in the room, as if to attention, were a girl and a woman. The woman was about forty, I reckoned, and was small and homely. She wore a dark brown dress with a faded yellow apron over it. Her skin was weather-beaten, and she wore a bright welcoming smile. Her hair was brown with wisps of grey and she had tied it back in a bun. She reminded me of the women from Uist, a sturdy farmer's wife. The girl, on the other hand, was unlike any other girl I had ever seen. Her skin was a tawny/brown shade, much darker than a Scottish person's skin. She had high cheekbones that gave her face a flat look and her hair was long and shiny black hanging loose to her hips. But her eyes were of the lightest blue and looked quite strange against the darkness of her skin. I shivered as she stared at me in a way that made it impossible for me to figure out what she was thinking. Suddenly she moved her gaze to Roderick and, to my astonishment, ran towards him, throwing her arms around him.

'Welcome back, *Athair*,' she said in the Gaelic. 'I've missed you.'

46

CHAPTER THIRTEEN

Athair? What the devil did she mean? I looked at Roderick, wanting with all my heart to ask him, but I held my tongue as he made the introductions after he had loosened the girl's arms from around his neck.

'This is Heather, my ward, and Amelia Bukowski, our nearest neighbour who has been looking after Heather while I've been in Scotland.'

'Pleased to meet you, Chrissie,' the woman said with a slight accent, and I wondered where she had emigrated from. As if she had read my mind, she continued.

'I come from Poland. Like your husband, the incentive that the Canadian government was offering to set up farms in the prairie lands attracted my husband, Aleksander. It is a good life, but a hard one. It can get lonely, so I hope we will become friends. Women need other women to talk with.'

I shook the woman's outstretched hand and liked the touch of her worn skin against mine. It again reminded me of the hard-working women from my homeland. There was something about the name Bukowski that I recognised and that was when I remembered the skeleton and blurted out before thinking.

'So, was it your husband who found the skeleton on the land he was ploughing Amelia?'

'Yes, but how did you know about that?'

'Bill at the Golden Sheaf told us. That must have been such a shock for him and you,' I said, wishing to hear about this discovery straight from the horse's mouth as it were, but Roderick interrupted.

'And this is Heather.'

'Yes, sorry Heather.'

I then turned towards the girl and held my hand out cautiously to her. Heather curtsied, took my hand, and shook it. Roderick smiled and offered me the explanation I was waiting for.

47

'Heather became my ward when her mother died and I'm the only father figure she's ever known. I taught her to speak the Gaelic and English and she speaks her mother's native language too. However, she needs help with reading and writing and perhaps you could help her with that.'

'Me? You mean she will continue to live here with us? I thought it would be only we two Roderick.'

Amelia coughed discretely and made her farewells, promising to ride over next week and see how I was settling in. After she left, the three of us stood awkwardly with the question I had asked hanging in the air between us. I was thinking of the long-suffering life with my sister Morag and hoped this young girl would be different. I didn't like the look of her. There was something of the savage about her, and as I studied the girl, the stories I had read of how the Indians had murdered the early settlers in their beds came into my mind. I shuddered. What if Heather's relatives came looking for her and attacked us? But worse than that, how would Roderick and I ever be able to make a go of our marriage with a young girl in the house. I was disappointed and wondered why he hadn't told me about Heather before I married him, or at least when he was telling me about Katie. It wouldn't have been such a shock now.

'Heather, would you mind fetching water so that Chrissie can have a bath after her long journey?'

'Yes, father,' she said, and left us alone.

Roderick sighed and took my hands in his.

'Now you wouldn't want to send a young girl away on her own, would you?'

'But why can't she go back to her own people. She must have other relatives she could live with. We passed an Indian Reservation on the way here, didn't we?'

'Yes, but she's not welcome there. Her father was a white man, and she has no male relative who could take responsibility for her. This means she cannot move back to the reservation. Besides, you know that I'll be away a lot looking after the farm and it means that Heather can keep you company.'

'Why didn't you tell me about the girl before we got here. You had plenty of opportunity.'

'I didn't want to put any more doubts into your mind, Chrissie. I knew it upset you when I told you about Katie and the arrangement with your father and I didn't want to add to your concerns.'

'I found the idea of having a family of my own hard enough Roderick but taking on some other woman's child is too much.'

'Think of the benefits of having someone to share the women's work of the farm with,' he said, smiling encouragingly at me.

I was unsure what kind of work Roderick would expect me to do here and had hoped that being a married woman would free me from that burden. I now realised it was a foolish notion when I remembered the rough skin on Amelia's hands and what Roderick had said on the ship about men needing women to help them run the farm. That made me think about Janet working as a maid in the big house. Maybe Heather could be like my maid, and I could be like Mistress Victoria. It would be pleasing to tell someone what to do rather than someone else telling me. Besides, I had no choice. I would just need to become used to this new life and this girl. It wasn't until I was lying in the tin bath that Heather had prepared for me I thought more about her mother. I wondered what role she had had in Roderick's life that had made him take on the responsibility of being her guardian. I would need to ask him, but uppermost in my thoughts was what would happen with Roderick that night. Would we consummate our marriage? I was prepared to do my duty, but I wanted to get it over with as painlessly and as quickly as possible.

Later, as we got ready for bed, I bit my lip and fidgeted with the buttons on my nightdress when Roderick interrupted my nervous thoughts.

'Chrissie. I have a present for you.'

'A present?'

'Yes. I wanted to give you something as a wedding gift, something that would be meaningful in our lives together.'

I stared at him, wondering what kind of present he was going to give me that would make our lives together meaningful rather than just a business transaction. He handed me a plush blue box and inside, sitting on the white quilted silk interior, was the most beautiful silver hairbrush and mirror I had ever set eyes upon. Taking the brush out, I fingered the soft bristles and touched the exquisite whorls worked into the metal.

'Thank you so much. They are beautiful.'

I felt tears nip my eyelids. I suppose if anything was meaningful between us, it was a hairbrush. I remembered how he would brush through my curls gently and how much I loved that time with him when I was a child.

'Just like you,' he said.

We looked at each other, neither of us smiling or saying anything for a few minutes.

'You know I was there on the day you were born? I had a job helping your father on the croft. I remember thanking my lucky stars that I wasn't a woman when I heard your mother's screams as you made your way into the world. When your father brought you out, I saw this little creature with a scrunched-up face yelling her head off. I'd never seen a new-born baby before and was awestruck.'

I kept quiet as I watched my husband's face, which was as expressive as it had been when he was describing tilling the virgin land.

'It was for this reason that I took an interest in you. I remember when you were a little older, I used to sit and brush your hair. You had wild curls that needed taming, and Marion insisted it be brushed 100 times every day. You used to like when I had a break and would sit with you brushing your hair slowly rather than pulling on it roughly the way your mother did.'

'I remember Roderick and I asked if you would marry me when I grew up because I liked the way you brushed my hair.'

50

'That's right, and I laughed. But when my father wrote to me about you, I remembered those times and I wondered what you were like now. I know I came back to Scotland to make you my wife because I needed someone to help me run the farm, but you are a beautiful woman that any man would be proud to call his wife. I am confident that in time we will learn to love each other.'

By this time, the tears that had nipped my eyelids were spilling down onto my cheeks. In all my dreams, I had never imagined a wedding night like this. I realised that those romantic stories that Victoria and I used to read were just so far removed from real life. He came close and wiped away my tears with his thumbs, and the feel of his fingers made me shiver.

'Don't be afraid, Chrissie. I will try not to hurt you and I will do everything I can to make you happy.'

He took my face in his hands and looked deep into my eyes. I noticed again, as I had on that day when he had saved me from Colin, that he had the bluest of eyes as he put his lips gently against mine. His kiss was tender, and his fingers explored my body so slowly and kindly that I could not help but respond to his touch. *Mathair* had been right. There was some pain initially, but Roderick awakened such desire in me, I hardly noticed it. Much to my surprise, I welcomed the feel of him between my legs and the sensations that it aroused in my body, so much so that when he let out a cry of pleasure, I joined in. I had never experienced joy like this and afterwards, when he cradled me in his arms, I cried like a baby. We were now truly husband and wife - the reverend McEwan would be proud.

It was late into the night by the time we settled down to sleep. I lay listening to Roderick's shallow breathing, feeling relaxed and happy for the first time since I had left home, until I heard a blood-curdling howl.

'What was that?' I screamed, shaking Roderick awake.

'It's alright, my love, it's only a coyote. You are safe here. You'll get used to them.'

51

But for the rest of the night, I could not sleep for the sound of the howling wolves and felt exhausted by the time dawn broke, and it was time to get up and begin married life.

CHAPTER FOURTEEN

Married life in Canada was anything but the life of ease I had hoped for. I found out quickly why Roderick felt it necessary to have a wife. A woman's existence in the prairies was one of toil. While the men worked in the fields from sunrise to sunset, it was the women's job to make sure they were fed. We cooked breakfasts, lunches and dinners for our husbands and the hands who helped them, baked bread and biscuits, looked after our children which sometimes was for 24 hours a day when sub-zero temperatures prevented them from going to school, looked after the house, fetched water and wood, took care of chickens, cows, horses, pigs and any other animal running around the homestead and went into town to collect supplies which could be a round trip of three to four hours. Sunday was the only day of rest, and although I had no children and had Heather to help me, I still thanked God that He had given us the Sabbath.

Although having Heather to help with the chores was a blessing, in the beginning it was also a curse, as she was moody and unamenable unless Roderick was about. I had thought my sister Morag was a troublesome teenager, but Heather was worse. She never offered me any help unless I asked her, which was difficult at first as, although I knew how my mother organised the work of the croft, I was unsure how to do it for a prairie homestead. Roderick naturally assumed that Heather would instruct me on what I had to do, but she never did. He therefore could not understand why sometimes there was insufficient food to feed the hands, why we ran out of wood to fill the stove, or there wasn't enough water for drinking and washing. Although he said nothing to me directly, I sensed his impatience with my shortcomings, and it hurt. Now that we were so much in love, I wanted to do my utmost to please him and be the type of wife he needed. So, I resolved to learn every aspect of being a prairie wife. Luckily, Amelia took on the role of mentor in the early months and taught me how to manage a household efficiently and eventually I got to grips with most things.

I still wasn't a great baker, and I wasn't a gifted teacher either. I dutifully tried to teach Heather to read and write, but I had little patience when she got things wrong. I couldn't help my negative feelings towards her. My prejudice towards Heather's difference I now recognise fuelled these feelings, as did the fact that she thought of Roderick as her father. As far as I was concerned, Heather was jealous of me, and I could sympathise with her a little. After all, she had had Roderick to herself for years and now I was the centre of his world, so it was only natural she would be envious of our relationship. Although Roderick chatted to us both when we had settled down after all the men had been fed and gone to the shanty, he always brushed my hair before bed. It was not only a relaxing ritual, but it displayed an intimacy between us that Heather was not a part of. We regularly went to bed early, partly because we were exhausted, but because we longed to spend time together on our own and to make love when we had the energy. I had completely forgotten that ours was not a love match and must admit to feeling rather smug about the way things had turned out.

My feelings towards Heather changed one day when I had become frustrated with her yet again when I was trying to teach her to read and write. It never occurred to me it might have been my style of teaching that was to blame. I blamed Heather.

'Why didn't you learn to read and write at school?'

'I didn't go to school. My mother and father taught me.'

'But why didn't you go to school? Surely it's compulsory for all children to attend school.'

Heather's eyes looked at the floor and I could see her biting her lip. It was something I did when I was nervous or worried and I wondered what she was about to tell me. Had she been disruptive? Had she just been unteachable?

'I went for a few months when I was about six, but the teacher and the other children were unkind to me.'

54

'Unkind? In what way?'

'The teacher told me I should wash my skin with carbolic soap.'

'Why? Did you not wash before you went to school?'

Heather's eyes began welling up, and I felt a pang of guilt at the way I was questioning her.

'She told me my skin was too dark and I must try to lighten it as only savages have dark skin and there was no place for someone like me in her school.'

It appalled me that someone could be so cruel, and for the first time I felt something akin to compassion for Heather.

'The children called me names and spat at me. My mother and father spoke to the teacher, but it made no difference, so they stopped me going.'

I knew how unkind children could be at school, especially if someone was different. Miss Victoria had been bullied at school because of her legs and that was why she had had a governess to teach her. At our school, the other children had laughed at Lachlan because he enjoyed poetry. I considered myself fortunate that no one had bullied me, although I knew what Master Colin had tried to do to me was a kind of bullying but for a different reason. I shivered when I thought about it. But poor Heather, to face such prejudice because of the colour of her skin. It was then I realised I wasn't being that different from her teacher and resolved at once to be kinder to her.

'I'm sorry Heather. That must have been awful for you. You are doing well with your lessons, considering. Let's begin again and I'll try to be more patient.' She smiled, and I gave her a hug. My heart melted when she clung to me briefly.

Luckily, my teaching improved when Miss Victoria began sending me the women's magazines we used to read together with her monthly letter from home. This was a much better way to teach a young girl to read and write than the stuffy old books that were on Roderick's bookshelf. Heather enjoyed looking at the pictures in the magazines of women dressed in a way that she had never seen before, as London and Paris Fashions were nothing like anything that she had seen women wearing in the prairies. I enjoyed looking at them too and the magazine, together with the letters from my mother and Miss Victoria, helped to keep me sane and to remind me that there was more to life than being a homesteader's wife.

CHAPTER FIFTEEN

The months passed, and I settled into married life well, although I still found it hard not to be frightened when I heard the cry of the coyotes at night. Roderick told me that the government paid the homesteaders to shoot them. This meant, he explained, that sometimes he and the boys would go away for a couple of days at a time on hunting trips when work allowed. He also warned me to always carry a gun with me when going into town just in case I was ever late back, as it could be dangerous after dark. I had always been back before nightfall, but I knew it might be different in the winter when darkness fell by late afternoon.

Heather and I settled into a routine and worked harmoniously together. She did most of the heavy work around the house like cleaning, laundry, fetching water and wood, looking after the horses that were so essential to the work of the farm and tending the little garden that I found out Lily, Heather's mother, had made. It was a blessing as it gave us fresh vegetables to supplement what was available in town and herbs that I had never heard of, but which Heather assured me had healing properties. I milked the cow, fed the chickens, did all the cooking and baking, and drove into town for the supplies.

When I wasn't working on the farm, I visited Amelia or Amelia visited me and we would chat over the telephone. I still couldn't believe we had a telephone in the house, but it was an absolute necessity in the winter Roderick told me when we could be snowed in. I also visited Jeannie when I was in town getting supplies, so felt happy that I was making friends. From the two women, I learned about the associations set up by women to ease the loneliness and improve the lives of the homesteader's wives, but so far, I had not felt the need to join any of them. I now had a horse of my own and had named her Clover after the pink clover that grew on the machair at home. She was a beautiful chestnut brown mare with an even temperament and she and I became close companions as I rode her most days. Having Clover meant I could visit Amelia or Jeannie whenever it suited me. I had never ridden a horse before coming to Canada and it was Heather who had taught me how to mount, sit and control her. Heather whispered a lot to the horses, but she never told me what she was whispering, but it sounded like it was in her mother's language.

I often thought about Heather's mother and how she and Heather had ended up living with Roderick. Amelia had told me that Heather and her mum had lived with Roderick for as long as she and Aleksander had lived in the area. In fact, it was Lily who had delivered her two children, as she was renowned for her skills in birthing babies and in providing remedies to help women who were with child.

'Her death has been a genuine loss in this community.'

'When did she die?'

'Just last year, a couple of months before Christmas. Roderick and Heather were devastated when it happened.'

I felt a pang of jealousy when I heard this. Why would the death of his housekeeper devastate him?

'How did she die?'

'She had gone into town for supplies. I remember that day as if it were yesterday. The morning started off clear and bright as winter days do, but before long, an early snow had fallen and within an hour, it had covered everything. You haven't seen the snow here yet, Chrissie, but it is a dangerous thing. It can bury a man or a woman in no time. When Roderick saw the extent of the snow, he phoned Jeannie to see if Lily had made it into town, but Jeannie hadn't seen her.'

'What happened to her?'

'She must have lost her way, as the snow had quickly covered all the tracks over. It looked like her horse had been injured as Roderick found her and Star the next day. There wasn't much left of them after the wolves had got to them.'

I shuddered. Poor Lily. I would not wish a death like that on anyone. No wonder Roderick had warned me about taking a gun and being home before dark, but I was unsure why he hadn't told me what had happened to Lily.

'She must have been so terrified. God rest her soul.'

Although I felt sorry for how the woman had died, it didn't stop me from wondering about Lily. Had she known the squaw who was married to Jim Adams? In my more imaginative moments, I even wondered if she had been his wife. The skeleton that Aleksander had found was one of my favourite topics of conversation. From what Amelia had told me, both he and his wife had gone missing, but Aleksander had only discovered one skeleton. That made me wonder whether it was his wife who had shot him and then run away. Whenever I tried to speak to Roderick about it, he would laugh at my ghoulishness and tell me I would make a wonderful author for the Penny Dreadfuls that had been popular in Scotland before he left. The poster that the Mountie had put up was still outside the post office, but the last time I had seen it, it was looking the worse for wear and I thought it would more than likely blow away in the next storm.

CHAPTER SIXTEEN

It surprised me, therefore, when one Sunday afternoon, I saw a Mounted Policeman riding up to the house. When I told Roderick, he looked annoyed.

'You go out and see what he wants, Chrissie.'

'Good afternoon Ma'am. Hope this isn't an inconvenient time to call,' said the Mountie, when I went outside.

'No, not at all. This is our rest day, so we are taking the time to relax. What can I help you with, sir?'

'Well, Ma'am, don't know if you heard a skeleton was dug up a short while back in one of the neighbouring homesteads. It had been there a long time, so we didn't think anyone would offer information, but they have.'

'Have they? That's wonderful. You might solve the mystery then.'

'Maybe. I'm hoping your husband, Roderick Macdonald, might help me. Is he around just now?'

'Roderick? Well, yes, he is inside. I'll just get him for you.'

I went back inside, and Roderick looked up from his newspaper.

'He wants to see you, Roderick. He says someone has come forward about the skeleton and he thinks you might be able to help him.'

'Right. You better ask him in for coffee then. Leave it to me to do all the talking, Chrissie. I don't want your overactive imagination getting in the way.'

When the Mountie was seated at the table with a coffee and one of my oat biscuits in front of him, Roderick asked him how he could help.

'We got a witness who says that you were in the Golden Sheaf around the time Jim Adams went missing. He swears he saw you talking to the man's wife, a squaw called Lily.'

'Lily?' I asked, despite what Roderick had told me.

'You know someone of that name, Ma'am?'

60

'Chrissie only arrived in Canada this year sir, so could never have met Jim Adams or his wife,' Roderick told the Mountie before I could answer, so I decided I better let him do all the talking as he had asked me to do.

It was hard for me to sit silently as my mind was running like a hare with all the possibilities surrounding Jim Adams's death, but I sat and listened intently to what was being said by the Mountie and Roderick.

'So, Mr Macdonald, can you confirm if what the witness says is true.'

'I'm afraid I can't. I knew Harold Winter, who owned the hotel before Bill Preston even though I very rarely went into the Golden Sheaf back in the days when it sold alcohol. I am a non-drinker sir and always have been. However, I did occasionally go in for a coffee, so it is possible I met this, what did you say his name was?'

'Jim Adams,'

'Jim Adams and his wife, but if I did, I do not recall it.'

'How long have you lived here Mr Macdonald?'

'About fourteen or fifteen years.'

'Just about the time that we reckon Jim Adams and his wife went missing.'

Roderick said nothing, just continued to gaze at the Mountie with an inquiring look.

'I hear tell you have a squaw and a half-breed child living with you, sir. Is that correct?'

'Well, not any longer. Wolves killed *Waskatamwi* a while back, but her daughter Heather does still live here. Why do you ask, sir?'

Waskatamwi. That wasn't Heather's mother's name. It was Lily. Why was Roderick lying about that?

'Well, it just seems a bit of a coincidence that you have a squaw living with you after a man is shot in the back and his squaw wife goes missing.'

'Did this Jim Adams have a child with the squaw then?'

'Not to my knowledge, but who knows. Where is she, by the way?'

'She's visiting with her friend Hannah, our neighbour's daughter, and won't be back until tomorrow.'

Another lie. Heather was due back this evening.

'What age is the girl?'

'I'm not right sure. She and her mother came to live here about ten years ago, and she was just a little thing then.'

'Ten years ago, hmm! So, tell me Mr Macdonald. How come you ended up with a squaw and her kid staying with you?'

'Well, I was betrothed to my wife, Chrissie, when she was just a child and had to wait until she grew up to marry her. We were married just three months ago in Scotland.'

Roderick looked fondly at me and squeezed my hand.

'I wasn't looking for a wife, but as the farm grew, I needed a housekeeper who could do the cooking and other things that are women's work on a farm. I put an advert up in the post office and in the Saskatchewan Herald, but I did not hold out much hope that I would find someone. As you know, there are no surplus women in these parts, so I was grateful when Heather's mother answered my advert. I gave her a trial to see if things would work out, and they did. The girl is still here because she's a good worker and helps Chrissie a lot, doesn't she, dear?'

I nodded enthusiastically.

'Right, well, thanks for answering my questions. I don't think we will need to take it any further. It is all so long ago now and according to our witness; he was a real bad'un and was cruel to the squaw. He probably deserved to get a bullet in the back.'

'Can I offer you another coffee, sir?' I asked him, although I was desperate for the man to leave so that I could find out from Roderick what all this was about and why he had lied to the Mountie.

'No, thank you, Ma'am. It is a long ride back to Yorkton, where I am based. You folks take care now.'

I didn't bother watching from the porch until the dust from his horse had disappeared before going back into the house as I normally would when we had visitors. I was too eager to hear what

62

Roderick had to say. He came over straight away and took me in his arms. His kisses filled me with desire as I felt the hardness of him against me. Normally, with Heather being away, I would have been more than happy to use this time we had together to make love. But not today. I needed answers and it couldn't wait. I pulled myself reluctantly from his arms.

'Roderick, I think we need to talk rather than make love, don't you?'

'Do we?' he said, trying to draw me into his arms again, and it took all my willpower to resist.

'Yes. I need to know why you lied to that policeman. Did you know this Jim and his wife? Was his wife Lily and was he Heather's father?'

'No, but Heather's mother was called Lily. I wasn't lying. Waskatamwi means Lily in Cree. I knew with your imagination that you would think she was his wife and had been involved in his murder. That's why I said what I did.'

'So, you thought he would be like me and put two and two together and make five.'

'Precisely,' he said, taking me in his arms again.

'And why did you say Heather wouldn't be home when you know she will be?'

'I didn't want her upset by someone asking her questions about her mother. She was very distressed when Lily died, and I didn't want it all raked up again.'

I hesitated, then I decided to believe him. Why would he lie? I went willingly with him this time when he took me in his arms and kissed me. We rarely got the house to ourselves, so it was a wonderful feeling to make love without worrying that Heather or one of the men would hear us.

CHAPTER SEVENTEEN

Harvest time was now over. The reaping, threshing, winnowing, and hauling of the wheat to the elevator had all gone according to plan, so Roderick and the hands finished it well before the first snowfall. I now understood how hard the men worked during harvest time and was pleased for Roderick when he told me he, Aleksander, and the hands were going on a hunting trip. I was also happy that Heather and I would have more time to ourselves, as we had worked extra hard during harvest, too. I was less cheery, however, when I woke up the day after he left feeling sick. Before long, I began vomiting violently into the commode.

'You're having a baby,' Heather said.

A baby. The thought warmed me, and I couldn't wait to tell Roderick. I was confident it would delight him to have his own child. And *Mathair*. I would need to write to Mother and let her know the good news.

'So how do you know that I'm going to have a baby, Heather?'

'My mother taught me lots of things and she told me that women stop bleeding and get sick. I noticed you had not bled this month and now that you are being sick, it is the only logical reason.'

'Aren't you clever? You don't talk much about your mother, Heather. Why is that?'

'It upset Roderick when my mother died. He never wanted to talk about what had happened to her, so I just stopped talking about her.'

'Would you like to talk about her to me? It helped me when my grandmother died to talk about her to my family. It kept her alive in my memory. She was the first person to die that I had ever known, and the thought of dying frightened me.'

'I wasn't frightened of dying, as it is the natural order of things, but I worried Roderick would send me away when he married you. I thought you wouldn't want another woman's daughter living with you.'

64

She had guessed rightly how I might feel, so I spent some time letting her talk about her mother.

'What was your mother like?'

'Very beautiful. She had the same colour of skin and hair as me, but her eyes were brown. She talked little, but you could tell that she understood lots of things. All the women around these parts appreciated her skills as a midwife and the medicines she made up to help them.'

'Do you remember anything about your real father?'

'Roderick is my real father,'

'Roderick's not your real father. I understand why you call him father, but your mother had you before you came to live here.'

'No, I have always lived here. First in the shanty where Frankie and the other hands live now and then in this house when it was built about ten years ago.'

'So, you remember living in the shanty?'

'Yes. I felt wonderful when we moved in here. There was so much space, and I could have a room of my own. The shanty just had one large room. Mother and Father slept in one bed at the top end of the room, and I slept in a smaller bed at the other end. We did all the cooking and washing there as well.'

'Your mother slept with Roderick?'

'Yes.'

'But I thought he employed your mother as his housekeeper, not his wife.'

'Yes, that's right, he did.'

I was silent as I took in the implications of what Heather had told me.

'Thank you for letting me talk about my mother, Chrissie. I'm going to visit Hannah now unless you want me to do anything.'

'No, no. You get going. Say hello to Amelia for me.'

When she left, I was restless and began pacing the floor. What did this mean? Had Roderick deliberately misled me the way he had misled the Mountie when he came to ask him questions. He had told the Mountie that Lily already had Heather when she came

65

to live with him ten years ago, but Amelia had told me that Lily had delivered her two children and her eldest daughter, Hannah, was about thirteen. He had also told me that Heather was his ward, and that Lily was his housekeeper, yet if Heather was to be believed, then she had been more than that. If they slept together, then Heather could be his actual daughter and not some other man's child, as he had told me. But worse than these things was the thought that my husband might be a murderer. What if it was him who had shot this Jim Adams in the back because he was in love with Lily and wanted her for himself? All my doubts about Roderick swept back in and my joy at finding out I was with child left me. I desperately wanted him to return so that I could have all my questions answered, but he was going to be away for another two days.

CHAPTER EIGHTEEN

It felt like the longest two days of my life. I was sick on both mornings and just knew that I was definitely going to have a baby. I hugged that happy knowledge to me but couldn't help the anger that was growing inside me towards Roderick. I wanted to get to the truth of things between him and Lily. For the first time, I felt homesick for my old life and my family. Life there seemed so much less complicated, but then I thought of Master Colin and knew that if he had had his way with me, my life could have been as difficult as this one. I could not get what Heather had told me out of my mind and was short-tempered with her. Nothing she did was right. On the day Roderick was due back, she made up a potion for me to take to help relieve my sickness, but instead of feeling grateful to her for trying to help, I threw the cup holding the potion at her and yelled.

'Keep your native remedies to yourself, my girl. I'll not be taking any of your poisons.'

'It's not poison Chrissie. My mother taught me how to make it. She gave it to Amelia and lots of the other women who were with child. It will make you feel better, I promise.'

At the mention of Lily, I became even more enraged. Poor Heather didn't know what she had done wrong.

'I said I don't want it. Can't you understand? Why don't you just leave me alone?'

Just then the door opened and there stood Roderick proudly displaying a bag of pelts from his hunting trip, but his face fell when he saw the heated exchange.

'What's going on? What's the matter?'

By this time, both Heather and I were in tears, and he stood looking at us in bewilderment. I turned on my heel and ran into the bedroom. I heard him asking Heather what was wrong and listened at the door to see if she would tell him I was pregnant.

67

'I don't know, *Athair*. I was trying to give her some medicine that Mama showed me how to make, but she accused me of trying to poison her.'

'What kind of medicine?'

'Something to help with an upset stomach. She has been sick.'

'I see. You have done nothing wrong, Heather. You were only trying to help. I'll have a word with Chrissie.'

I moved away from the door so that he wouldn't know I had been listening.

'Hello, my darling,' he said, coming over and taking me in his arms. 'Tell me what's wrong. Heather says you've been sick. Are you feeling better now?'

'I'm fine. I'm going to have a baby, that's all,' I blurted out.

His face lit up. 'A baby, but that's wonderful.'

As I saw how delighted he was at this news, I was sad that I had told him so bluntly, but my sadness didn't last long.

'So, why were you annoyed with Heather? She was only trying to help you. She learned a lot from Lily, you know.'

His words stung. He was taking Heather's side against me and had the cheek to mention that woman's name. I pulled myself free from his embrace and began my tirade of suspicions.

'And just who was her mother, Roderick? '

'What do you mean, Chrissie? I don't understand.'

'Well, let me explain,' I said, roughly wiping the tears from my cheeks. 'You led me, and the Mounted Policeman who questioned you, to believe that Lily and Heather only came to stay here ten years ago, but Heather told me she has always lived here and that you are her father, not her guardian. She also told me you slept with her mother.'

He had the good grace not to deny it, and I continued as his face grew ruddy with what I assumed was shame.

'So, it's true then. I would really like to understand why you lied to me and to that Mountie. Have you also lied about Heather? Is she your actual daughter and a half sister to this child that I am

68

carrying? Did you murder Lily's husband so that you could bring them to live with you?'

I could see the dismay on his face at my bitter words. I had never spoken to anyone like this before, except perhaps when my mother and father had told me about their plans to marry me off to Roderick. It was all their fault. If they hadn't promised me to Roderick, I wouldn't be in this predicament now. I suddenly became conscious of Heather standing at the bedroom door and turned on her.

'Get out of here. I'm having a conversation with my husband.'

Heather looked to Roderick as if for instructions, and he nodded. She left the room, banging the door loudly behind her. Damned half-breed. I didn't want her to be a half-sister to my child. I didn't want Roderick to have been in love with Lily. I didn't want to be married to a murderer. It was all too much to bear, and I collapsed onto the bed, crying and sobbing.

Roderick at once knelt beside me, whispering soothing words.

'Come on now, sweetheart. Let me explain. It's alright. It's alright. I will tell you truth and you will see it's not as bad as you think.'

But I wasn't in the mood to be sweet-talked into anything by this man who was a stranger to the truth. How could I believe anything he told me now?

CHAPTER NINETEEN

'I don't want to hear your lies, Roderick. I cannot bear to look at you. I'm going out for a ride.'

'You can't Chrissie. It's almost dusk, and it looks as if it's going to snow. You won't be safe.'

'Worried that your wife will end up like your mistress?'

I could see how my words stung him, but I couldn't think about him now. I had to get out of this house, or I would go mad. Ignoring his pleas, I shoved past him and pulled on my outdoor clothes. Heather was standing near the door but said nothing, for which I was grateful. The sky was heavy with grey clouds, but there was still some daylight left. I prepared Clover and mounted her with a heavy heart. I clicked my tongue and urged her forward with no idea of where I would go. All I knew was that I had to get away from Roderick and have some time to think on my own. I was no longer a silly little girl who could have a tantrum if she was unhappy about something. I was a married woman who had made vows to live with my husband till death separated us. How could I break those vows? Were there actions by a husband that justified ending a marriage and would what Roderick had done qualify as one of those actions? Murder was a serious crime and one of the ten commandments that as Christian people we must follow. He must have really loved Lily to have murdered her husband. Did he love me now as he professed or was he just trying to make the best of a marriage that provided him with a wife who could help him run the farm, someone to warm his bed at night but not someone that he truly loved. I was overcome with jealousy and disappointment, and the more I went round and round in circles in my head, the more I urged Clover on. Time disappeared, and I didn't know how long I had been riding for when the first snowflakes fell.

I pulled on Clover's reins and stopped, searching the horizon for a landmark that would tell me where I was. But I recognised nothing. I gazed skywards as thick snowflakes landed on my eyes and lips, their icy texture melting on my tongue. I had never seen so much snow and was mesmerised by its beauty as it fell in large silent flakes from the dark sky to cover the sleeping landscape. Its white blanket hid the night and lulled me into a false sense of well-being. This changed and fear gripped me when I realised that the snow had covered the tracks that Clover and I had travelled along, which meant I wouldn't be able to retrace our path. I thought about Lily and how she had died and as if on cue, I heard the first night chorus of the wolves. Without my gun, I would be powerless against them. I thought of my baby lying dormant in my belly and prayed as I imagined the coyotes feasting on it after they had picked the flesh from my bones.

'Oh God, please, please let me find my way home. Don't let the wolves get us. I'll do anything you want,' I bargained. 'Just don't let me die on these prairies alone.'

I wondered if Clover could find her way home by instinct and tried this. I gave the mare her head, but she stood still at first, moving her head and nickering quietly, the warm air blowing from her nostrils in white clouds. Then she turned and ambled slowly along the soft snowy ground as if trying to get her bearings. Eventually she trotted, but the going underfoot was difficult as the snow continued to fall, creating deep drifts. I had heard about Canadian winters and how the snow could bury a horse and its rider in no time.

A lethargy grew over me as the cold and dampness seeped through my clothing into my bones. My hands and feet were numb despite the fur mitts on my hands and the heavy woollen socks I wore under my boots. The wind rose, and the snow blew in gusts against us until I had to lie almost flat against Clover's back. Suddenly, she stopped, and I almost fell off. Exhausted and hemmed in by snow, my poor girl could go no further. I knew I could not go on foot, so I climbed off Clover's back and tried to create a hollow in the snow where I could hunker against Clover's body to keep warm and hope that help would come before we both died. Despite our argument, I had no doubts that Roderick would try to find me, but would he be able to?

I don't know how long we lay there before I heard a sound in the distance. The snow had stopped falling, and the night was clear and crisp. Clover whinnied and her ears went up as she heard it, too. Roderick was coming for us at last. Thank you God. It was then that I noticed a pair of bright eyes glowing in the darkness – a wolf. It was circling us, calculating whether it could attack. I pressed against Clover and pulled myself to my feet, looking over the ridge of snow to see if I could see anything. My heart soared with hope as I saw a light swinging in the distance and a horse pulling a buggy on a sleigh. Sitting on top looked like a man and a girl. It could only be Roderick and Heather.

'Roderick,' I called out, but my voice was a croak against the wall of snow. I waved my arms frantically, hoping that they would find us before it was too late, but by that time I was so exhausted I had to give up and sink down into the hollow of snow again. The wolf was now on the other side, above where we huddled. It was moving in for the kill.

Unexpectedly, I remembered when I was a young child and scared I would sing. Somehow it made me feel less frightened, so that's what I did. If ever I needed comfort, it was now. I sang a working song that *Mathair* and I would sing together when we were milking or churning the butter. As I sang, I could have sworn my mother was singing along with me. Little did I know that the sound of the sweet song would guide Roderick over the snow to where Clover and I lay. I could see the wolf's eyes directly above us now, but kept singing, fixing my gaze on the wolf. The song stuck in my throat as I saw a flash and heard the boom of a gun just before the wolf fell on top of Clover, who neighed and tried to shake it off in alarm. A sloshing sound drew near, and I could hear Roderick and Heather calling my name. I called back in relief and gratitude. God had answered my prayers.

I don't remember too much about that night, I was so disturbed by what had happened. All I know is that Roderick saved me, took me home and tucked me up in bed with a hot whisky and extra blankets to heat my shivering bones. When I woke in the morning, my heart began to beat faster when I realised Roderick was not lying by my side in our bed. Where was he? Had he left me? I cried as I remembered what had happened the night before. How could I have been so stupid; going out like that, despite Roderick's warning. I was a lucky woman not to have died out there. But then I remembered why I had left the house.

'Roderick,' I called. 'Where are you?'

The door opened, and he stood in the doorway, blocking the light. Was I married to a murderer? I felt afraid at the thought.

'I'm here Chrissie. How are you my darling?'

He strode into the room and sat down on the bed, taking my hands in his.

'Roderick, I need to know if you are a murderer. How could I live with a murderer? How could I tell my child when he or she is born that their father is a murderer?'

'Hush, hush *mo ghraidh*. I'm not a murderer. Please let me explain and you'll see things are not as bad as that imagination of yours is making them. He then told me all about Jim Adams, Lily, and Heather.

CHAPTER TWENTY

'That first time I set eyes on you, when I was driving along in the buggy from the pier at Lochmaddy and saw Colin pulling at you, I was straightaway reminded of the first time I met Lily. I had not long arrived in Canada and was trying to find my feet. The little town of Saltcoats was just springing up with the new settlers coming into the area to claim their pieces of land from the government and I was full of high hopes for the future. It had been a big decision to leave home, but there was little on the island for me. The land available for crofting was becoming less and less and I had heard that Canada was a thousand times bigger than the Hebrides and that there was land going for free. The opportunities were endless. All I had to do was find the money for the fare for my passage. When your father offered to pay my and Katie's fares as a kind of dowry, I jumped at the chance. Unfortunately, as you know, things didn't work out with Katie, and I came on my own. But to get back to my story.

I was in Saltcoats picking up some supplies when I heard a man shouting at a girl and pulling her towards him.

'Come here, you savage.'

She was crying and speaking in a language I did not recognise. I had seen several natives since I had arrived and had been quite frightened at first as I had heard all the horrible stories of fighting between them and the early settlers and how savage they were. But nowadays, the fighting was at an end and the natives were living in settlements set up especially for them. The men came into town to trade just like anyone else, so it surprised me to see a girl who seemed to be on her own. I was even more surprised to see that no one was paying any attention to the fact that the man was roughly handling her.

'What's going on?' I shouted over at the man.

'None of your business. Butt out Scotsman.'

'I'm making it my business,' I said, strolling over towards the man, hoping I looked braver than I felt. I'm not a fighting man

Chrissie, but I couldn't stand by and do nothing when someone was in trouble.'

'She's my wife, one of the mail order variety.'

'Mail order. What do you mean?'

'You really are a green neck, aren't you?' the man sneered. 'Just wait till you've been stuck on your farm with nothing for company but the sound of the wolves, and you'll be looking for one yourself.'

I still didn't fully understand what the man was talking about.

'But the girl clearly doesn't want to go with you,' I told him.

'No, she doesn't, does she,' he said, giving the girl a slap causing her to cower and whimper like a dog, 'but I've paid good money to that agency for her, so she's mine.'

He then lifted the girl up on to the back of his saddle and rode off with her, much to my shame that I could not help her.

I was determined I would not be like that again, and that was why I intervened so readily when I saw Colin pulling at you. My thoughts went back to Lily, who had not been so lucky as I hadn't been able to save her. At least not then. It was a few months later that I bumped into her and her husband again in the town. I now knew what mail order brides were and why some men went for them. I wondered if I could wait until you grew up Chrissie or whether I would succumb to the posters advertising women to marry.

It was a freezing bitter day when I saw Lily standing outside the Golden Sheaf Hotel. She was standing beside a buggy dressed like the other prairie wives, but her hair was still hanging loose as I had seen her that first time. Although she had a fur skin draped over her shoulders, she was obviously freezing as she was stamping her feet and flapping her arms back and forth to keep warm. As I approached her, I saw the man who had married her staggering out of the hotel. It sold liquor in those days. He grabbed her round the waist and kissed her on the mouth. She did not resist, but she did not respond either. As I stood looking at them, the man suddenly threw her aside and looked towards me.

'What are you looking at, stranger? Never seen a man kiss his wife?'

'Sorry. Your wife looked so cold standing there. I was about to go over and see if I could help her. It must be well below freezing today.'

'It sure is,' said the man. 'Where you from, stranger? I haven't seen you in town before.'

'I own a homestead up Mackenzie way. I rarely come into town, but I needed some supplies before the heavy winter weather closes in.'

'Jim Adams,' the man said, holding out his hand.

'Roderick Macdonald,' I said, taking the man's hand. It was rough and dirty. I could smell the whisky on his breath. I am a strict teetotaller as you know. I had made my mind up before I left for Canada that I would live a clean life and save all my money. I suppose I wanted to show Katie that I could make a success of my life without her.

'Why don't you come in and have a drink with me, Roddy. It'll heat your bones for the drive home.'

'I don't drink, sir, but I don't mind coming in and having a coffee. Perhaps your wife should come in too. Get her out of this cold.'

'You seem a bit too concerned about my wife. You not got one of your own at home?'

'No, but I am betrothed to a girl back in Scotland and I plan to bring her over here and marry her someday.'

'Lily's fine, anyway. She's used to the cold. It's in her blood.'

The man swaggered over to the woman, took her arm, and pulled her after him into the hotel. I followed them in and was glad of the warmth. The woman sat in a corner of the bar while her husband ordered himself a whisky and a coffee for me. He had no sooner drunk his whisky down than he had ordered another one until finally he was so drunk he wanted to fight with anyone who was up for it. As often happens when men drink to excess, there was a brawl, and they threw tables and smashed bottles and glasses all over the place. I could see Lily cowering in the corner

76

trying to avoid the bodies and bottles that were flying around and went over to take her out of the melee.

'Take your hands off my wife,' Adams roared, 'or I'll kill you.'

When I turned, I saw that the man had a gun in his hand pointed right at me. I did not carry a gun, although I had one back at my cabin in case of wolves or bandits, but oh how I wished I had it with me now.

'Let's all calm down now,' Harry the bartender said, holding a shotgun in his hand. 'I think it's time you and your missus went home Jim.'

'Oh, do you now? Think you're a big man with that big gun in your hand, do you? I'll go when I'm ready and I won't be ready till this Scotsman leaves my wife alone.'

'I was only trying to stop her from getting hurt in the fight Jim. Come on now. I'm going to get my provisions, so I'll see you next time I'm in town. Yes?'

I turned my back on him, but every nerve in my body was tense with fear as I made my way towards the door. I heard the gun being cocked and braced myself for the shot, but when it came, it wasn't me who fell. I turned to see what had happened and saw that the bartender had shot a hole right through the middle of Jim. Lily wailed, a shrill unearthly sound. It was a sound I never wanted to hear again.'

CHAPTER TWENTY-ONE

'When Lily's screams subsided, there was silence until Harry broke it by walking back to the bar and hanging his gun up above the gantry. It was an excellent incentive for the hard men who came into the bar not to misbehave, but then men like Jim Adams had no common sense and let the drink steal their brains so that they could not think straight anymore.

"Get the Mountie Scotsman," Harry called to me. "He'll know what to do with the body and his wife. The rest of you get on home"

The bar cleared quickly, no one wanted to get into trouble with the Mounties who were a law unto themselves. As far as I was concerned, they were more like mercenaries than the constables I was used to in Scotland, and I wasn't sure how they would deal with this situation or indeed with Lily. Without thinking it through, I made Harry an offer. I don't to this day know why.

"Look, Harry, I don't want any part of this. He brought this on himself and if it's the woman you're worried about, I'll take her home with me. I could do with some female company." I winked and tried to laugh like a man of the world. "I'll even dispose of his body for you. What do you say?"

"Well, if you're sure. It would certainly save me a lot of problems trying to explain to the Mountie what happened".

"I'm sure. If it hadn't been for you, I would have a bullet in my back, so I owe you my life."

"Alright then. You better get going before anyone goes and tells the law themselves."

I turned to Lily, who was sitting totally still. She was obviously in a state of shock.

"Do you understand English?" I asked.

She looked at me with dull eyes and nodded.

"Your husband is dead. I am going to take him and bury him on his homestead and then I am going to take you back with me, together with anything that is worth saving from your home. Is that acceptable to you?"

She nodded again.

"Do you have anything I could wrap his body in? I don't want to be seen driving off with a dead body in full view."

"Pelts in the buggy," Lily suddenly spoke in slightly broken English. "You cover him."

It was my turn to nod. I went outside, made sure there was no-one on the street, then Harry and I carried Jim out to his buggy. It was full of animal pelts, and it was easy to conceal him.

"Can you drive the buggy?" I asked Lily, and she nodded again. She was a woman of few words. "I'll follow behind you. Are you sure you want to come home with me? I won't hurt you."

"You are a kind man," she said. "Thank you."

CHAPTER TWENTY-TWO

'I remember how hard the ground was as I tried to dig a grave for Jim. The snow had fallen, and I knew from what it was like the first year I had arrived that the temperatures were going to be almost unbearable. It was a relief to have so many pelts to help keep us warm. I dug as fast as I could so that we could get away before the snow trapped us. When I went into the homestead, Lily had everything packed up and was ready to go. She was quiet. She didn't utter a word, just looked at me. I wondered what she was feeling. Was she upset about Jim being dead, or was she relieved? I suspected it was the latter. It was unlikely that he had been kind to her. By the time we reached the shieling, the snow was so high that we had to dig ourselves into it.

I remember how pleasant it was to have someone with me, even if she said little. She set about finding her way around the shanty, which wasn't hard given that it was only one large room, while I lit the fire so that we could get some heat into us. I already had some rabbit stew, so Lily heated this up and we had it with chunks of bread and hot black coffee. The shanty had two beds in it, a double and a single. The extra bed was there in case I hired someone to help till the land, although I had hired no one so far. I told her she could have the double and I would sleep in the single bed. She looked at me with a puzzled expression but got her things together and climbed into bed. That night was the coldest I could remember since I had come to Canada, and I shivered in bed despite the blankets from home and the fur pelts from Jim's hoard that I had piled on top. I realised the shivers were probably as much to do with the aftershock of seeing a man killed at point blank range, burying him, and taking his wife home with me.

As I lay trying to sleep, I could hear Lily moving about. She was obviously having difficulty sleeping too. I could hear the spark of logs from the fire and realised Lily must have sat there instead of going to bed. I decided to join her, but as I pulled my covers back, her slender figure was standing at my bedside. She was naked and her hair was loose. I felt my body responding despite what my head was saying, so that when she came to me, I couldn't resist. She whispered to me in her own language, then in English told me she was scared that the spirit of her dead husband would come to haunt her and could she sleep with me. I don't believe in spirits, but I understood how she felt. Just at that moment, there was the terrifying sound of howling from the wolves. She let out a yelp and clung to me, and I clung to her. Before the night was over, we had become one. I knew I was sinning, but I couldn't help it. As a mere man, I hoped God would understand my needs.

Lily and I got on well. She still talked little, but gradually I could sense that she was more relaxed and that she trusted me. She was always considerate, making sure I had food to eat when I came in from work and that the cabin was clean. She didn't seem to mind that I was out working all the time and spent the hours on her own setting up a vegetable and herb garden. She explained to me about the medicines that she could make from the herbs, and she became well known in the community for her remedies.

A couple of months after Lily moved in, I heard her being sick a few times. When I asked her if she was ill, she told me she thought she was having a baby as she hadn't bled this month. For a moment, I was excited at the thought of becoming a father, but then realised that the baby could also be Jim's. I would never know, but I vowed to look after the child as if it were my own. I thought about my family back home and the arrangement I had made with your father to return and marry you. I knew my family would disapprove of this turn of events, so decided not to tell them. Scotland was so far away; it was unlikely that I would ever see any of them again.

In terms of the arrangement with your father, I knew he had only offered your hand to me because of his shame over what happened with Katie, and he probably didn't believe that I would come back for you, anyway. As far as everyone else around here was concerned, Lily had been pregnant when she came to live with me, and she was merely my housekeeper. I didn't avail them of the fact that she was more.

And that was how I ended up with Lily living with me and how I gained a daughter.'

CHAPTER TWENTY-THREE

'It doesn't change how I feel about you, Chrissie. I love you with all my heart. These last few months since you came here have been the happiest of my life.'

I was in a daze at his revelations. How could he say it wasn't as bad as I had imagined? The only thing he wasn't guilty of was murder. My emotions veered between admiration that he had saved Lily from that monstrous man, horror at him covering up a murder and burying the body and jealousy that he had lived with Lily as his wife and didn't know if he was Heather's father. A heavy silence hung between us for what seemed an eternity, but I could think of no words to say that would express how I felt. Even my tears had dried up. He had turned my world upside down; everything I thought I knew had changed.

'Why didn't you marry Lily?' I asked eventually.

'I don't know. I think perhaps you were always there at the back of my mind as the woman I would marry.'

I felt myself softening. What had happened to me last night had given me a different perspective on life. Everything wasn't black and white. No person was all good or all bad, and I knew in my heart that Roderick was a good man and would do everything he could to make me happy. But my hope that we could resolve the rift between us flew like a feather with his next words.

'Besides, she was registered as being married to Jim and if we had tried to marry, it could have opened up many problems. We didn't register Heather's birth for the same reason.'

'So really, you were just trying to cover up Jim's murder. Not that you didn't love her or want to marry her.'

As I looked at him, I wondered if his actions had been so bad. He had only tried to help a woman in trouble. But that woman had been Lily, and he had clearly had feelings for her. He was my husband, my betrothed since I was five. How could he have gone with another woman? I knew I was being irrational. I hadn't wanted to marry him and had even harboured thoughts of marrying Colin

83

Donaldson, but it made no difference to the searing jealousy that swept through my body now.

'I'm so sorry, Chrissie. Please, please don't leave me. I love you more than life itself.'

'How can I believe anything you tell me now? You're not the man I thought you were Roderick, and I don't know what to do about it. I'm stuck here thousands of miles from my home, from my family and am having a child with a man who is a liar and a sinner.'

My harsh words surprised me. I sounded like the minister when he was ranting at the congregation about sin.

His face was ashen, and his eyelashes were wet with tears at my cruel words, but my mood was dark, and I felt a cloud of disappointment and sadness envelop me.

'Where would I go? I will stay with you, but I do not know if we can ever be truly husband and wife again.'

CHAPTER TWENTY-FOUR

I dreaded the nights now. After my ordeal, I either couldn't sleep or when I did, I had nightmares. The nightmares were the worst. I dreamed constantly of the coyotes ripping my baby from my stomach. I hated leaving the house and refused to go into town for supplies. Heather did most of the outside work, but Roderick thought she was too young to go into town on her own so asked Amelia if she would help while I was ill. Roderick had sent for Dr Munro to look me over but the injuries I had were not physical. I could not free myself from the dark sadness and fear that shrouded me. It was as if God had abandoned me. He had taken me away from my home and everyone I knew to live in this strange land and like the Israelites, I could find no song to sing in it. Life held no hope. I was little more than a mail order bride, someone brought in to help my husband to run the farm and I wasn't even very good at it. My underlying fear was that I would be no good at being a mother either. I couldn't speak of my fears to anyone, especially not Roderick. We hardly talked to each other these days and there was no hair brushing or love making. The doctor recommended rest for a couple of weeks, but the weeks turned into months.

It was January and about four months into my pregnancy when things changed. I had taken the potions that Heather had made me to help with morning sickness, but she also gave me something to help with my anxiety and at last it seemed to work. But the most significant factor in my recovery was the day I woke up and felt the stirring of life within me. It was like a little breath; a featherlight flutter in my belly. My shroud lifted and hope filled me as I thought of this new life growing inside me. I must pull myself together for this child. I could not abandon it to live without me in this brutal land.

So, I rose, dressed, and set about preparing breakfast. Normally Roderick was away to work by the time I appeared, but this morning he was the one still lying in bed.

'It's good to see you up and dressed at this time, Chrissie,' he said, when he followed me through. 'Are you feeling better, my love?'

'I think so Roderick. I can't explain. I just feel so much lighter, like a huge load has been lifted from me. I'm sorry I've been so morose these last few months. Can I have a hug?'

'Of course, my sweetheart,' he said, coming over and folding me in his firm embrace. I realised how much I had missed our closeness. 'Those pancakes smell good.'

'Tuck in. There are plenty.'

Heather came and sat at the table.

'I think our Heather has had something to do with my feeling better.' I smiled at her. 'Those herbs she's been giving me have worked a treat.'

Heather blushed, but I could see that my praise pleased her.

'Things are going to change around here now. I'll be pulling my weight again. It might take me a bit of time to go into town on my own, so I would appreciate Heather if you would come with me to begin with.'

'Of course, Chrissie. When would you like to go? I'll phone Amelia and let her know you are feeling better.'

'You're a good girl. Thank you. How about tomorrow?'

That night Roderick brushed my hair again. When he had finished, I took his hand and laid it on my tummy.

'I felt our baby today, Roderick. Can you feel it?'

Placing one hand gently on my stomach, he sat gazing into my eyes, waiting to sense this little miracle. Tears fell from his eyes as he felt a movement.

'I felt it Chrissie, I felt it. Heather, come and see if you can feel him too.'

I was sad to notice how Roderick looked askance at me, no doubt fearing he had done the wrong thing by inviting Heather to share this special moment, so I smiled and beckoned Heather over. She was part of our family, and it was only fair that we should include her.

86

'I can feel him too,' beamed Heather.

'Him? Do you two know something I don't?'

'Och, I don't care if it's a boy or a girl, so long as he or she is healthy,' said Roderick, kissing me softly on the lips.

I knew how much Heather had done during my illness and was grateful. None of what had happened was her fault. She was an innocent child, and I was glad that Roderick was the sort of man who would shelter and care for a child even when he wasn't certain if she was his. I could also understand how lonely it must have been for him, all alone in the shieling in the middle of nowhere. Anyone would crave company living out in the wilds like this, so I was glad that he had found Lily to look after him. It was now my turn to look after him and I would do so to the best of my ability. I was ready to let go of the past and move on to the next chapter of my life.

On the night that our son was born, it was Heather who helped me. It was a beautiful June evening when little Roddy entered the world. Everything went smoothly. Heather had coached me in breathing techniques that her ancestors used, and she had also given me one of her herbal remedies to help with the pain. It was painful. I couldn't deny it, but it was like my mother had told me, I forgot the pain as I held my baby in my arms. As I looked at my son, I vowed to always be there for him, to cherish and nurture him so that he would grow up to be as kind a man as his father.

Roderick had been pacing around outside during the birth, but when he heard the baby cry, he rushed in. Heather had wrapped him in a calico blanket, and she handed him now to Roderick.

'He is beautiful, Roderick, and he looks just like you,' she said.

'He is indeed beautiful, but I think he has Chrissie's lips and nose.'

Turning to me, he looked at me earnestly and smiled widely.

'Thank you, Chrissie, for this wonderful gift. There is not a man alive happier than I am at this moment.'

I knew this to be true, as his face beamed with pride when he looked at the bundle in his arms.

'What shall we call him?'

'I think we should call him Roderick after his father,' said Heather.

'I think so too,' I said, smiling and taking her hand. 'Thank you *mo ghraidh* for everything.'

So, we named him Roderick Angus Macdonald, Roddy for short.

'Let us say a prayer together over our son,' Roderick said, taking mine and Heather's hands in his and together we asked God to bless him and give him good fortune all the days of his life.

IN SICKNESS AND IN HEALTH

Canada 1912

CHAPTER TWENTY-FIVE

It was just after little Roddy's first birthday when Roderick became ill. It came on suddenly. He had been tired, but that wasn't unusual, as work on the homestead farm was always tiring. But he also had a persistent cough, which he shrugged off, impatiently telling me he was alright when I said I wanted to call the doctor in to look at him. Until he collapsed. Doctor Munro arrived promptly and within five minutes had diagnosed tuberculosis. It was the word that everyone dreaded hearing, as it caused as many deaths as typhoid in the province.

'What will happen, doctor? Will he need to go to the hospital? I've heard the Anti-Tuberculosis League is looking at setting up sanitoriums like they have in Europe.'

'You're right but, unfortunately, Mrs Macdonald there are no sanatoriums in Saskatchewan yet and it will be a couple of years before they build any. I would recommend that your husband sleep in a different room from you and that you serve his meals separately. I'll leave you some cod liver oil and make sure he gets out in the fresh air as much as possible. That should help his lungs.'

'How long for, Doctor?'

'I don't know Mrs Macdonald. I've known of some people who have been in hospital for a good number of years and of course you need to face the fact that half of those people who develop symptoms will die.'

I felt myself grow cold. The thought of Roderick dying was unthinkable, so I put it from my mind and thought about the immediate situation. How would we manage? We had Frankie, Hamish and Jake, who worked on the farm, but Roderick told them what to do and did as much work on the farm as they did. Who would bring in the harvest? We depended on the harvest for our livelihood, a good or bad one could make or break us.

'I can't emphasise enough, Mrs Macdonald, that you, your baby and your, err,' he said, looking at Heather, 'maid will need to keep your distance. Living with someone who has consumption can mean that you become infected too.'

'How do you think Roderick became infected, Doctor?'

'I don't know. It's possible he picked it up on the ship that you travelled to Canada on. It can lie dormant for several years before any symptoms appear. You know that there are new laws about spitting and Roderick should give up his pipe. Clean fresh air is the most important thing for your husband now, and rest, of course. I'll call in from time to time to see how he's getting on, but if you need me, just get a message to me and I'll come over.'

I glanced at Roderick and could tell from the way he was looking at me he knew it was bad news. I felt guilt sweep over me at how angry I had been with him when I found out the truth about Lily. If the worse were to happen, I would never forgive myself for being so cruel to him. Determined not to let him see my fear, I smiled brightly once the doctor had left.

'So, it's lots of rest for you, *mo ghraidh*. The doctor thinks you have the consumption, but he says with plenty of cod liver oil and clean fresh prairie air, you will be right as rain in no time.'

'There's no need to spare my feelings, Chrissie. I know the statistics for tuberculosis, but I promise you I will fight it with all my might. I have everything to live for and I shall pray to God to have mercy on me. So, what do I have to do, Chrissie? We can't continue to live as closely as we have been.'

'No, you're right Roderick. I'm afraid you will have to live in a separate room and keep as far from us as you can. I think the best thing is if you move into Roddy's room and we move his cot in with me, as our room is bigger. We can set up a table and chair for you to have your meals in that room and outside we will set aside the south side of the porch only for you to sit so that you get the sun in your face.'

'But how will you manage? The hands are rough and need a man to keep them in line and you are still feeding Roddy.'

'I know that Roderick, but it's more than that. You do the work of two men, so we will need someone to replace you too if we are to get the harvest in on time.'

'Maybe Aleksander could help.'

I thought he would be busy enough getting his own harvest in now that he had the Adam's homestead as well as his own to worry about. I decided not to say anything though as Roderick's breathing was becoming more laboured by the minute and he fell back on the pillow.

'I'll just make the bed up in Roddy's room and you can move through there. Then I'll get these sheets off and boiled to make sure none of the germs are lingering. Heather is keen to see you. Shall I send her in?'

'Yes but tell her not to come too close. I don't want to spread it to her. Chrissie, you will be kind to her, won't you?'

I smiled, trying not to feel annoyed. Heather and I had been working amicably together for the past year, so he had no reason to ask me that now. Was he never going to let me forget how unkind I was to her when I first came? But my annoyance left me as he began coughing and I remembered how precious he was to me.

'Yes, of course. She was the one who delivered our little Roddy safely, and for that I shall be forever grateful. I'm sorry I was so unkind to her before. I was jealous, I suppose, of your relationship, but I realise now that there is more than enough love for us all.'

CHAPTER TWENTY-SIX

After I had settled Roderick and the baby into their respective new rooms, I decided I better speak to the men. Heather told me they had asked her why the doctor was visiting, so they obviously knew something was wrong. The men didn't take too kindly to me telling them that their boss had tuberculosis. I could see that they wanted to up and run, but they knew if word got round that Roderick Macdonald had the consumption, then they wouldn't find it easy to get another job as people would think they might carry the disease too. I noticed they stood well back from me.

'We will put an advertisement in the Post Office and in the newspaper for someone to take over while Roderick is ill but, in the meantime, I'll be looking after things.'

There was much murmuring and shuffling of feet.

'But you don't know the first thing about raising grain, Ma'am,' said Frankie, 'with respect,' he added, removing his hat.

'I know Frankie, but Roderick will keep me right until we get a replacement and besides, you are all so good at your job, you need little supervision.'

Frankie and the others didn't smile, so I knew my try at flattery hadn't worked.

'At least we'll get a fair rate for our crop now that Roderick is a member of the Cooperative Elevator Company.'

I now tried to make them think I understood the politics of farming by mentioning the elevator company, but I only knew that it had been a problem in the past because of Jeannie. Roderick never spoke to me about the farm business apart from the things which involved Heather and me. It was Jeannie who had told me that before the Cooperative had been set up, the private companies who had owned the elevators had exploited the farmers.

'You're right Ma'am at least that's something you don't need to worry about now. Those scoundrels used to pay the farmers a pittance, keep the grain sitting in the elevator until the price rose and then they sold it for a sizeable profit.'

'I'm looking to make one of you up to foreman until I can find someone to work here on a full-time basis to cover for Roderick. I'll pay extra wages.'

The men looked towards Frankie, who, although he was young, was the obvious leader of the three.

'I think we men need to have a chin wag about this Ma'am and we'll get back to you,' he said.

I nodded, turned on my heel and went back to the house where Heather was waiting for me.

'What did they say, Chrissie? Are they happy for you to be the boss?'

'Not really. They don't think I'm up to it and quite honestly, I don't think I am either.'

'What about a foreman? Who came forward?'

'No one yet. Frankie is the obvious person for the job, but he's trying not to be too keen. Said they need to have a chin wag about it, and they'll get back to me.'

'Well, you know you can count on me to do anything that is needed. I'll support you and Father in whatever way you want.'

I still bristled a little inside when Heather called Roderick Father, but I didn't show it. She had proven her worth, and over the last year, I had grown fond of her. She was so good with little Roddy. Luckily he was now able to be fed with formula as well as breast so she could help with feeding too which would be a huge help if I was to take on supervision of the men. We both enjoyed reading the magazines that Victoria still sent from home and discussing the latest fashions. I now realised that my life would have been completely different had Heather not been living with us, and I was grateful for her.

The next day I rode into Saltcoats. I was parched when I arrived and went straight to the Golden Sheaf. The place was empty.

'Hello, anyone home?' I called out.

'Hello Chrissie. Lovely to see you. Come on in and sit. Coffee?' said Jeannie, coming through and rubbing her hands on her apron.

'Something cool, please. I'm thirsty. The trail was very dusty today.'

'Is something wrong Chrissie? You're looking tired and worried if you don't mind me saying,' she said, as she passed over a glass of lemonade.

'Well, I am. That's why. I didn't think it was so obvious though.'

'Tell me what's wrong. What's happened?'

'It's Roderick. He has the consumption.'

'Oh no!'

I could see Jeannie's face go pale and she involuntarily stepped back from me and who could blame her.

'That's the worst news. I'm so sorry to hear that. What are you going to do?'

'Well, we are setting the house up so that we can separate him from Heather, Roddy and myself.'

'Yes, it would be awful if he passed it on to any of you.'

'He isn't too bad just now and hopefully we'll have caught it early enough for him to recover. We can't send him to one of those sanatoriums as there's none in Saskatchewan yet, so he needs to stay at home.'

'But we're coming up to harvest. How on earth are you going to get that gathered in?'

'Well, that's one reason I've come into town today. I've got a notice to put up in the post office and I'm putting an advert in the Saskatchewan Herald.'

'I see. But how will you cope in the meantime and what will you do if there isn't anyone?'

'That doesn't bear thinking about Jeannie. I've told the men I want one of them to be the foreman until I can get someone to cover for Roderick so they are discussing it today and will get back to me tonight.'

'I hope they don't prove awkward, Chrissie. '

'Me too. And obviously, if you know of anyone yourself who you think would take on this job, you will let me know.'

'Yes, of course. Look, I'll contact my friend Rose at the Homemakers' Club and tell her your news. They have a group of women who help families who have someone infected with tuberculosis.'

I wondered what kind of help they could offer but I would be grateful for anything that would make things easier.

'That would be good. Thanks Jeannie. Right, I better get on. Thanks for the lemonade. Don't forget to let me know if you can think of anyone.'

CHAPTER TWENTY-SEVEN

That week was a busy one for me. I hardly drew breath what with looking after Roderick, cooking for the men, trying to give them instructions and riding out to check on how they were getting on. I thanked God more than once for Heather, who looked after Roddy and helped with all the other chores that needed done. The men had chosen Frankie to be the supervisor as I thought they would, but he had told me that if I didn't get someone to replace Roderick, they wanted a share of the crop money. I thought this was fair, given that the men would need to step up and do much of the work without supervision and the cost of hiring someone to replace Roderick would work out around the same amount.

I hadn't discussed this with Roderick, as he was in no fit state. He was weak and could barely walk from his bedroom to the porch. His cough was still persistent, and I had a continual knot in my belly. Would I be able to run this farm on my own if we couldn't find someone to replace Roderick? It was hard enough doing the chores that Heather and I had to do to keep things going but working with the men was a whole different matter. Although they were polite enough, I could see that they didn't respect me. I felt like they were a pack of hungry wolves circling me, just waiting for me to make a mistake so that they could pounce. What that would mean, I had no idea. The only thing I knew for sure was that I needed someone I could trust and someone who knew the business as well as Roderick did.

Towards the end of the week, I spotted a buggy with two women approaching the house. I didn't recognise them and wondered why they had come. I was in no mood for visitors and expected they would run a mile if they knew tuberculosis was in the house. Thinking they might be lost, as it was unusual to see women visiting a homestead who weren't neighbours or friends, I went out to greet them.

'Good morning ladies. Have you lost your way today?'

'We sure hope not. Are you Chrissie Macdonald?'

'Yes. How can I help you?'

'We're hoping it's us who will be able to help you.'

I thought they must be travelling saleswomen wishing to sell me something, although I had only ever seen men doing that type of work. In fact, the man who had tried to sell Roderick the Kodak camera had come back a year later, and I had talked Roderick into buying one. He was always very careful (some would say penny-pinching) with his money, but I had convinced him to part with his hard-earned dollars by pointing out that we could take photographs of little Roddy to send home to North Uist so that our families could see what he looked like.

'Help me? How may I ask?'

'Sorry, we should have introduced ourselves,' said the older of the two, a stout woman with a large bosom trapped in a tight-fitting jacket and a plump cheery face under her bonnet.

'I am Rose Graham,' said the younger of the two, jumping agilely down from the buggy, 'and this is Fanny McGregor.'

She extended her hand to help her friend step down, and they continued together.

'We are from the Homemakers' Club.'

I remembered Jeannie saying that she would talk to her friends in the Homemakers. I had heard of the Club as it was the talk of the women in Saltcoats last year when the University of Saskatchewan had set it up. They had done so following a women's conference and there was much excitement amongst the homesteaders' wives. Lots of women, including Amelia and Jeannie, had joined it, but I had never found the time.

'Why don't you come sit on the porch, have some tea and you can tell me why you're here. I'll ask my ward to look after your horse and buggy.'

When Fanny and Rose were seated, I asked Heather if she would mind tending to the horse and I could see the usual puzzled expression on their faces as they wondered how a half-breed Indian girl could be my ward.

98

Glancing over to Roderick, who was sitting on the far side of the porch, I called over to him and introduced the women.

'Roderick, these ladies are from the Homemakers Club.'

'How do?' he nodded.

When I came out with a tray holding tea and scones, the women began to talk. They were relentless, one talking immediately after the other so that I couldn't get a word in.

'We are from the Homemakers' Club, Mr Macdonald. Rose and I are on the Committee of the Yorkton Branch and it's our role to reach out to homestead women to offer them any help that we can,' Fanny called over to Roderick.

'Yes, we know how difficult and lonely it can be for the wives. In fact, we're surprised that you haven't joined us, Mrs Macdonald,' said Rose, addressing me.

'It was Jeannie who told us about you, Mr Macdonald. We understand you have caught tuberculosis,' Fanny again called over to Roderick.

'And that's something we can help you with. We have supplies of sputum boxes and disposable cheesecloth handkerchiefs for you to use,' continued Rose, again looking at me.

'And we can have your place disinfected if need be,' said Fanny, now addressing me also rather than Roderick. 'Yes, it's our job to teach you all about how to deal with this terrible illness.'

Luckily, they stopped to drink their tea and munch a scone, so I could have my say.

'That's very kind of you. Any help you can give us will be welcome, won't it Roderick.'

He nodded again. It was too much of an effort for him to say anything.

'What about the cleanliness of your house? Do you regularly disinfect Mr Macdonald's room and bedding?'

I felt myself becoming defensive. Who did they think they were, coming in here and questioning my ability to care for my husband?

'Of course. Heather and I are very conscientious in that respect. Roderick has his own room and eats his meals separately

99

from us. He has spent the last few weeks since he became ill, sitting in the open air on the porch. I think we are doing fine here ladies.'

I could see Fanny and Rose looking at each other and raising their eyebrows. Then, as if in silent communication, they rose as one from the table.

'We did not mean to offend you, Mrs Macdonald,' said Rose. 'We can be a little overzealous sometimes.'

'Yes, but only because we want to do our damnedest to fight this disease,' said Fanny.

Turning to Heather, she then asked if she would bring their horse and buggy to the front.

'We have a supply of the sputum boxes and handkerchiefs in our buggy so we will leave them with you. Just contact us when you need more,' said Fanny.

'And we'll also leave you some leaflets which explain all about the Homemakers and about tuberculosis,' continued Rose.

'It was very nice to meet you, Mrs Macdonald,' they then said in unison.

'Please do consider becoming a member,' said Fanny. 'We need young women like yourself to join us oldies.'

'Thank you for coming and for bringing the boxes and the handkerchiefs. They will be a great help and I promise I will think about joining you,' I said, feeling relieved that they were going.

CHAPTER TWENTY-EIGHT

A month had passed since I had put the notice up in the post office and in the newspaper, but I had received no inquiries and was beginning to despair. Then Jeannie telephoned with news.

'Hello Chrissie. There's a young man from Scotland staying in the hotel. He just arrived on Monday. He's here in response to an advertisement that Aleksander Bukowski put in the paper for a hand but when I told him about your situation, he said he might be interested.'

'He wasn't put off by Roderick having the consumption?'

'Didn't seem to be.'

'What is he like? Do you think the men would take instruction from him? They certainly don't take too kindly to taking orders from me.'

'Well, he is young, only mid-twenties, I reckon, but he's one of those confident men who has an air of entitlement about them that makes you believe they can do anything. He told me he worked with his father and uncle in Scotland and has a wide experience of farming and agriculture.'

'I suppose he's worth a try. When is he due to begin working with Aleksander? I better interview him as soon as possible. I don't want him to leave Aleksander in the lurch, but I think our need is greater, don't you?'

'I sure do, and the Bukowski's will understand. They're your friends.'

'Can I come to the hotel tomorrow and interview him? I would rather see what he's like before I tell Roderick.'

'No problem. I'll check what time suits him and telephone you back.'

There wasn't much time to worry about meeting the young man as there were so many other things to worry about, so I set off the next day with hope in my heart that he would be just the person we were looking for. My hopes were instantly dashed when I saw who it was.

'Master Colin? What are you doing here?'

'Hello Chrissie, nice to see you too,' he smiled.

'You two know each other,' said Jeannie. 'Well, what a coincidence.'

'Yes, Master Colin was the brother of the woman I was a companion to back home.'

'Well, it's a good thing that you already know each other. It will be easier for you to decide, Chrissie. I'll leave you to your interview. Just let me know if you need anything.'

'Thanks Jeannie,' I said, smiling faintly at my friend while my brain raced. Knowing him did make it easier for me to decide. The answer was no. There was no way that Roderick would ever agree, but I had arranged this interview, so I better go ahead with it. However, it was Colin who spoke first, making me annoyed at myself that I had let him take the initiative.

'So, Chrissie, tell me what's happened. I hear your husband, Roderick, is it, has the tuberculosis. He was a powerful man that day we ran into him at the market. He sent me away with my tail between my legs, that's for sure. I'm sorry about that. I hope I didn't hurt you.'

'You scared me more than hurt me Master Colin.'

'Call me Colin. I'm not anyone's master anymore.'

'Why are you in Canada? Aren't you supposed to be at the military academy?'

'After what happened with you, my father and I argued. The result was that when I left Sandhurst I couldn't return home so came here.'

I would need to let Victoria know. She said in her last letter that they had heard nothing from Colin since he had fallen out with their father. As he was talking, I wondered if he was the same horrible person he had been back home or had he matured, like me.

'But what brought you to Saltcoats? Did you know we were here?'

'No, not at all. I came over to Canada with a friend as I liked the sound of it and applied for several jobs when we got here. I've been working my way round the various farming areas of Canada. I just answered an advertisement as I wanted to do more work on the prairies. To be honest, I would have avoided this area if I had known you and Roderick were here.'

'And do you like Canada? It differs greatly from North Uist.'

'It certainly does, but I must say, I like it. I love the wide-open spaces here and it is so good for growing wheat and other arable. Which brings me to the reason for our meeting today. Jeannie says you need someone to help you run the farm while Roderick is ill.'

Again, I had let him take the initiative. What was wrong with me?

'Yes. I've just appointed a foreman, but the men don't enjoy taking orders from a woman. Also, I don't know as much as Roderick and unfortunately, he's not in any fit state to educate me in the ways of farming. I really need someone who can run the farm.'

'Well, I obviously don't have as much experience as Roderick, but I know how to handle men and I could learn what I need to quickly. Shall I come out and see your farm and get a feel for the scale of your operation?'

I hesitated. My first reaction was that I would tell him he wasn't suitable, but what if no one else applied?

'Look, I'll need to discuss it with Roderick first, so I'll contact Jeannie tonight and leave a message for you. Can you come over tomorrow if he agrees? I really need to get things sorted.'

'Yes, I can see that.'

His look of sympathy told me I was giving too much away, but I had no experience of negotiating. That was men's work.

'Tomorrow's fine.'

'I better go. My baby boy will be needing fed.'

'You have a baby now. What's his name?'

'Roddy after his father.'

'Well, wish Roderick well from me and I'll hopefully see you tomorrow. But don't feel bad if he doesn't want to take me on. I understand and I'll still have the job with Mr Bukowski.'

As I rode back home, I tried to figure out what I was feeling. Was Colin trustworthy? He seemed a changed man, but could a leopard change its spots. Was it just a front? Would he make a play for me again, knowing that Roderick was ill, and I had no one to protect me now? I thought about the silly girl I had been two years ago and decided to give him the benefit of the doubt. If I could change, then so could he. I would just need to convince Roderick.

CHAPTER TWENTY-NINE

I thought about Roderick as I rode home. I knew how helpless and hopeless he felt lying in bed when there was a farm to run, but the cough wracked his whole body and sapped all his energy. He could hardly make it to the commode, and he was always apologising for being a burden to me and Heather.

'You would both be better off if I were dead,' he would say, but would then ask God to forgive him for having such thoughts when Heather would burst into tears.

'Don't talk like that Roderick. You know how much we love you,' I would say, but I knew the darkness of depression and how hard it was to overcome it.

'I know you love me and would do anything for me. I'm sorry. I not only have you two ', he would say, trying to smile, 'but a young son who will need a father growing up. I'll survive this Chrissie, don't you worry.'

'I know you will. You just have to keep going and do what the doctor tells you,' I would say when he was in this frame of mind.

Doctor Munro and the women from the Homemakers had been good at coming by and telling us the latest news about the treatment of Roderick's illness, but they told us nothing that was life changing. I wondered how he would greet this news that I was bringing about Colin, but I knew within my heart that he would not take the news well.

When I arrived home, I quickly jumped off Clover and led her into the corral. I knew I looked the way Roderick liked with my long fair hair pouring down from my hat and when I glanced over at him, I could tell in the way he looked at me he ached to be close to me again. Oh, how I ached for that, too.

'I'll just get us a cold drink and bring it out,' I said, smiling hello at him.

We sat in silence sipping our iced tea, my face in shadow as I braced myself for telling him my news and in the end it was Roderick who broke the silence.

'How was your trip to town? Did you and Jeannie have a good chat?'

'We didn't as it happened,' I said, turning to face him. 'I actually had a meeting with a guest at the hotel who Jeannie thought might be able to come and work for us.'

'Why didn't you say? That's great news.'

'Well, you may not say that when I tell you who it is.'

'Well, don't keep me in suspense.'

'Colin Donaldson, the brother of Victoria, the woman I used to work for as a companion back home.'

Roderick's face grew even paler than it was, and his voice was quiet.

'You mean, the man I had to rescue you from the day I arrived back in North Uist? The man who left a bruise on your wrist?'

I nodded.

'My God, does he think we would take him on to work for us. We may be desperate, but we're not that desperate.'

Roderick's anger made me wary. I would need to think of a way to make it acceptable. To make it so that he would approve of what I was doing because as far as I was concerned we were desperate.

'He has a lot of experience, Roderick. He worked with his father in North Uist learning the role of Factor during his holidays from university and he has been working here on farms for the past two years, learning all about Canadian farming. He believes this is a land of opportunity for those who are willing to work hard.'

'That's true, but he didn't seem the type of youth who would work hard. He seemed more like a lad who wanted something for nothing.'

'He says he's changed, and he apologised for what happened that day. He was young back then and he seems more mature now. Why don't I get him to come over tomorrow and you can see what you think of him yourself?'

He gazed at me, sucking on his pipe, which was empty of tobacco now, but which brought him comfort and allowed him time to think before answering.

'Yes, alright, but I'm not convinced he's the one for us. He may have gained some valuable experience over the last couple of years, but he still won't be as experienced as Frankie and the others.'

'I know, but he's a different class, isn't he? And in the military academy, they would have taught him how to tell people what to do. I think the men will respond to him better than to me.'

'Don't talk to me about class. I came to Canada to be a free man. Not to be beholden to those with money and title.'

Roderick's face was now hot with rage. I realised I had said the wrong thing and changed the subject.

'You're looking really hot, Roderick. I think I'll get some iced water and give you a sponge down now. Would you like that?'

He nodded, and I was pleased that he had allowed himself to be side-tracked from the subject as he lay back in his chair. I was also foolishly pleased that I had got him to agree to Colin coming over the next day.

CHAPTER THIRTY

Colin arrived early the next day on Jeannie's bay and I must admit he looked handsome in his loose white shirt, brown silk fronted waistcoat and brown trousers. A wide brimmed brown cowboy hat covered his head and his high leather boots were polished shiny black. Heather and I went out to greet him. Roderick was already settled on the porch in preparation for the meeting.

'Hello Chrissie. Could your servant see to my horse? The ride out here will have left him parched. It is quite a way from town, isn't it?'

'Heather is not our servant. She is our ward.'

'Sorry my mistake.'

'I'll take your horse, sir,' said Heather, smiling at him. 'You go with Chrissie, and I'll bring you a drink. I'm sure you're thirsty too.'

As Heather took his horse, she patted it and spoke to it in her native tongue as I had seen her do countless times. Colin looked bemused.

'What's the girl doing?'

'It's called horse whispering. It's something that her people do to calm their animals.'

'How come you have a half-breed as a ward.'

I could feel my hackles rising at the use of this term. Although it was in common usage, I found it offensive. Why call her a half-breed? Why not just call her a girl? But then I remembered the unkind words I had called Heather back when I had discovered that she might be Roderick's daughter and felt myself blushing at the memory. I was no better than Colin.

'It's a long story. Let me introduce you to Roderick before I take you around the farm and to meet the men.'

Roderick looked old and tired, sitting in his rocking chair on the porch. He was pale and thin, a shadow of the man he used to be, and I could see the shock on Colin's face when he saw him. He stayed well back from Roderick and took the chair furthest away from him. I sat closer to Roderick as I wanted Colin to see that I was a loyal wife and for Roderick to feel supported, but I still sat at a safe distance.

'Colin's here Roderick. I thought you would like to hear what he has to say.'

'How do?' Roderick nodded curtly.

I could see he wasn't going to make this easy.

'Hello Mr Macdonald. It's good to see you again. First, let me apologise for my behaviour that last time we met. I was a callow youth and thought I could do just as I pleased. I'm older and wiser now. Perhaps you would like to know a bit about me and what I've been doing since I last saw you.'

'That would be helpful.'

While Colin ran through what he had been doing, I couldn't help but admire his forthrightness in coming straight out with what was bothering Roderick and dealing with it head on. As I listened to his story, I thought he had grown up, and he had obviously learned a lot about farming. To my surprise, he told Roderick that he had come to Canada hoping to make a new life from himself away from the old ways of Scotland, which he could see were unfair to the local crofters. I wasn't sure that he was being genuine, but I hoped this would endear him to Roderick, who was as avidly anti-lairdship as my father and mother. When Colin finished, he gulped down the cold drink that Heather had brought him and sat quietly, waiting for Roderick to respond.

'Well sir, it would seem you have the necessary experience, but you will need to have a look over the farm and meet the men. I will then need to discuss the matter in private with my wife and she will give you our answer tomorrow. Thank you for coming and speaking to me directly.'

He coughed, and Colin rose quickly and moved back. While I understood his fear of catching the consumption, I wished he could be a bit more discreet in his revulsion.

'I'll take my leave of you now, sir,' Colin said, putting his arm up to cover his face.

After I had shown Colin round the farm and he had talked to the men, he rode off back into town. By this time Roderick was back inside in his room, sitting in a chair with a blanket around him. We looked at one another in silence, and I wondered what he was thinking. Could he let the past go and just see Colin for what he was now? Could I? At last, I could stand the silence no longer.

'What are you thinking Roderick?'

'I'm thinking he knows what he's doing and if he was anyone else, I would be happy to hire him. But he's not anyone else. He's Colin Donaldson.'

'He was good with the men, and he thought the size of the farm was a reasonable one for him to manage,' I said, hoping to help him see the positive side of Colin.

But when I looked at his face, I kept quiet. If I supported Colin too much, he might think that I had feelings for him and that would make him reject Colin for the job. I thought it best to let him talk it through in his own mind without me trying to influence him. He was my husband, and I would do as he wished.

'I can't get the image of him pulling you at the market out of my mind Chrissie and I'm afraid he may try to insinuate his way into your affections.'

'Roderick, I'm not a silly girl any more looking for romance. I'm a mother now and it's you I love. Don't you trust me?'

He looked at me with rheumy eyes and coughed into his handkerchief. I silently thanked Fanny and Rose for bringing a supply of the handkerchiefs that I could burn rather than re-use after boiling. It made life much easier and safer.

'I'm not much of a husband now, Chrissie. I can't do the work I need to do to keep you and our son safe and I can't give you the love and affection that a woman needs from her husband.'

'It's only for a wee while, Roderick. You'll be back on your feet before you know it, and this will just be a terrible memory.'

He looked at me, his eyes shining with tears and love.

'Alright, Chrissie. I trust you. I know you won't let him become more than just a hired hand.'

110

I truly believed that Colin would be only a hired hand in our household and that I would never be tempted even if he showed me affection, so it was with a light heart that I phoned the hotel and left a message for Colin that the job was his. I felt that an enormous burden had been lifted from me and thanked God for it. I also prayed that all would be well, but it was one of my prayers that He didn't answer.

CHAPTER THIRTY-ONE

After I had telephoned Colin to let him know our decision, he telephoned me back to ask about accommodation. I couldn't answer him as we hadn't thought about where he would stay. I agreed it was too far for him to travel in from town every day and that even if there had been enough room in the shanty for him to share with the men, it wouldn't have been proper given that he was now their boss. When I discussed it with Roderick, we agreed that the only other way was for him to move into the house. It wasn't an ideal solution, but we had space in the basement where we could make up a bed for him, so that is what we did. Colin living in the house with us worked out well as he was out most of the day supervising and labouring with the men. After his evening meal, he went to the basement to read and sleep, although on a Sunday we invited him to stay and play a game or just chat. If we were to keep him until Roderick was well, we had to make his life more than just working, eating, and sleeping.

Colin spoke to me much more than Roderick did about the running of the farm, and I gradually came to understand about the seasons and the work needed to keep the land working efficiently. The men liked Colin, and the dinner table was always a jolly place when they arrived in from work, with much laughter and good-natured teasing. I sometimes felt as if I was abandoning Roderick, who ate all his meals separate from us in his room. It was no life for him and the only topic of conversation between us now was his health. He usually fell asleep when I tried to tell him what was happening on the farm or my involvement in the Homemakers which over the last couple of months had become a lifeline for me. The women came to help Heather and I each month with disinfecting Roderick's room and bedding, bringing fresh supplies of the cheesecloth handkerchiefs and just chatting about what was happening in the outside world. I was grateful for their help, but life was hard and the drudgery of it all overwhelmed me sometimes.

So, it was with a feeling of excitement and a sense of freedom that I looked forward to the end of harvest celebrations which took place in November. All had gone well with the harvest. We had made a good profit, which meant there was enough to pay Frankie extra money for the short time he was acting foreman, to pay Colin's wages and to make a profit for the farm. There was to be a dance in the Golden Sheaf and Roderick had said that Heather and I should go in with Colin and the other men. That way, we would have protection and I wouldn't need to worry about travelling in the snow. I still suffered the occasional nightmare from my ordeal last year.

Heather and I giggled together like a couple of schoolgirls when we were getting ready for the dance. Heather was now fifteen and her body was filling out. She looked beautiful in her new red dress, with her long dark hair tied back with a red ribbon. I couldn't help a slight feeling of envy that Heather was young and free, well as free as a half Indian half European could be in our white European society. However, when I looked at myself in the mirror, I was happy with my reflection. Although my blue dress was more becoming of a married woman and I had caught my hair up in a net at the nape of my neck, the excitement of the night ahead had brought colour to my cheeks, and I felt pretty. How I wished Roderick was well again and able to admire me and tell me how beautiful I looked. I so longed to be held and to be made love to again.

Amelia had offered to look after little Roddy for the night and Roderick was settled in bed when we left, so we didn't need to worry about anything. We could just go out and enjoy the party and I could barely remember the last time I had felt so excited. The trip into town was trouble-free and cheery. The men were in high spirits, and I wondered whether they had been drinking the moonshine that circulated in the temperance areas, but I didn't care. I was going to enjoy myself and forget about my responsibilities for this one night.

CHAPTER THIRTY-TWO

When we arrived at the Golden Sheaf, it was jam-packed with men and women from all over the district, all set on having a good time. Jeannie and Bill welcomed everyone and told them to help themselves to the food and the hot and cold drinks that they had laid on. A band was setting up and the music would begin once everyone had eaten. I circulated, chatting to people I knew and even those I didn't know. Aleksander had come in with Hannah, so she and Heather linked arms and giggled together as they surveyed the room, no doubt full of excitement at attending their first dance. As I was nibbling at some food and looking round the room, Colin came over and told me how beautiful I looked.

'Thank you,' I said, feeling flattered despite our history.

When the band struck up and he asked me to dance, I went into his arms willingly and he led me into a waltz. We danced as if it was something we had been doing together forever and I would have danced with him all night if I could, but I noticed Heather standing on her own, looking over enviously at Colin and me. Hannah was on the floor with Jake, but it looked like no one had asked Heather to dance and I wondered why. I hoped it wasn't because she was half Indian. She was a beautiful girl that any man should be proud to have on his arm, and it was not that unusual for European men to mix with and even marry the native women. As Colin and I danced together for the third time, I asked him if he would mind dancing with Heather.

'I'd much rather dance with you,' he said, pulling me a touch closer to him.

I could feel the heat of his hand through my dress and the whisper of his breath on my cheek and had to admit that I wanted that too, but I had to remember I was a married woman and poor Heather was looking thoroughly miserable. When the band announced that the next dance would be a Dashing White Sergeant, it gave me the excuse I needed to draw Heather onto the dance floor with us. Heather and I danced on either side of

114

Colin as we *pas de basque'd* and twirled round the room in ever faster circles until we had to stop to catch our breath. When the dance ended, Colin moved on and began chatting with the lads from the farm while Heather and I fetched ourselves a drink.

When the music struck up again, Frankie came up to us and asked Heather if she would like to dance. She hesitated for a second, but then nodded and took Frankie's outstretched hand. I was relieved and wondered if Colin had asked the boys to take turns of dancing with her. I didn't like to see Heather standing on her own. It was the worst thing for a young girl. I remembered my experience at the ceilidhs we had back home. It was always nerve-wracking waiting to see if the boys who walked around eyeing up the girls like they were farm stock at the market would choose you. Janet and I used to moan about it and wondered why girls had to wait to be asked by boys and not the other way around. As I stood tapping my foot in time to the music, which was now a square dance, I gazed round the room and wondered which man I would ask to dance if it was the other way around, but I could honestly say there was no one there who attracted me.

I went outside for a breath of fresh air as the room was stiflingly hot. I had to put all my outer garments on again as the temperatures were so low at this time of year, they could freeze your hair. Many of the men shaved their beards in the winter for this reason. It was bitterly cold, and I shivered, pulling my coat tightly around me. I wished I could stay in the hotel tonight rather than make the long journey home in the cold and dark, although I had to admit it was a beautiful night as I gazed up at the inky sky which was bright with glistening stars. The light from the moon bathed the town in an ambient light accentuated by the whiteness of the snow and made the streets look almost pretty. I knew that although it looked beautiful and benign, the weather was unpredictable and there could be a further fall of snow or even a blizzard. So, I was glad that we were going home with the men and not on our own. Although all the runner tracks had now been cut through the snow which in some ways made it easier to travel

115

in winter than in summer on the dirt tracks, I couldn't forget that night when I had been lost and had almost become prey for the wolves.

'Hello,' said Colin, interrupting my thoughts.

'Hello.'

'Would you like a drink of hot punch? It will warm you up.'

I took the cup he handed to me and put it to my lips. Its warm sweetness pleased my taste buds, and I gulped it greedily.

'Here have this one. I haven't touched it. I can see how much you enjoyed that.'

'No, no, you have it. It's yours Colin. I'll get another one soon. Isn't it a beautiful night?'

'Almost as beautiful as you,' he said, his white teeth smiling out at me reminding me of a wolf.

'You are kind Colin, but I think there are many women inside who are more beautiful than me, and it is they you should compliment, not an old married woman like me.'

'But it's you I want to compliment. It's you who, if you were free, I would want to dance all night with. It's you I would want to take home. It's you I would want to kiss and make love to.'

I could feel the heat rising to my cheeks and as I gazed into Colin's eyes, my heart thumped, and my head throbbed. I felt as if I might faint and grasped his arm to steady myself.

'Sorry Colin, I feel rather lightheaded. I think we better go inside. This kind of conversation is inappropriate.'

He took my hand from his arm and held it in his, then bent down and kissed me gently. It had been so long since Roderick had kissed me that I responded. His lips tasted as sweet at the punch he had brought me, and I wanted so much to feel that sweetness on my lips, to feel his tongue searching for mine, to drown myself in his touch. But I also knew it was a sin, and it was then that God intervened.

CHAPTER THIRTY-THREE

'Chrissie, Chrissie,' called Hannah. 'It's Heather, she's being sick. We were dancing around and having fun with Frankie, Jake and Hamish, then she just turned deathly pale and vomited.'

I pulled away from Colin and ran into the room where Heather was. The poor girl was sitting on a chair with lots of people gathered round her. When she saw me, she jumped up and threw herself into my arms.

'Oh Chrissie, I don't know what's wrong. I feel so odd. Can we go home please? I want to go home and see father. I don't want him to be on his own,' she sobbed, huge tears running down her heated cheeks.

'It's alright. Don't worry about Roderick. He'll be safely asleep in bed by this hour. It's you we need to think about just now.'

Putting my arm around her, I drew her gently out of the room. Jeannie was standing watching us.

'I think it would be best if she had a lie down, Chrissie. She'll be alright once she has a sleep. I have an empty room you can have.'

When we got Heather into the room, we helped her off with her dress, which was now soiled. She was still sobbing quietly and was like a rag doll, allowing us to do as we would with her. I washed her face and brushed her hair, then helped her on with one of Jeannie's nightdresses. As soon as her head hit the pillow, she was asleep. I ran my hand softly over Heather's hair and sighed.

'What do you think happened, Jeannie? You don't think she's caught the consumption, do you?'

All my anxieties had returned.

'I think it's more likely that she has had some moonshine.'

'Moonshine? No, she wouldn't take that. She knows that Roderick and I are dead against alcohol.'

'I don't mean she's taken it willingly. She was fine until she drank the punch.'

117

'The punch?'

An image of Colin smiling his wolfish smile and handing me the warm glass of punch came into my mind, and I remembered how I had felt hot and light-headed after drinking it. I also remembered how my inhibitions had been lowered and had almost allowed Colin to kiss me. 'Do you mean someone has laced the punch bowl with alcohol?'

'No, not the whole bowl, as other people don't appear to be having any side-effects. I think the lads from your homestead have put it into the girls' drinks as a joke, but Heather has obviously had an adverse reaction. It's said that the Indians cannot tolerate alcohol in the same way as us.'

'Och, poor Heather. What an end to her first dance. Thanks for your support, Jeannie. Can I help clean up downstairs?'

'No, it's alright. Bill has already done it. Thanks. I think it's safer if you stay with her just in case she's sick again. People can choke, you know.'

So that was how I spent the post-harvest celebrations of 1912. I hardly slept for worrying about Heather and the feelings of shame and guilt that overwhelmed me when I thought about how much I had enjoyed the feel of Colin's lips on mine and how much I had wanted to return his kiss. I couldn't believe I was tempted, especially when I had promised Roderick faithfully that I would never be attracted to Colin. When I did eventually fall asleep, I had nightmares about Colin making love to me and Roderick crying and trying to pull him off. When I awoke at first light the following day, it was to smell of stale vomit and a crying Heather.

'Oh Chrissie, I can't remember much about last night after I had the punch. All I remember was dancing with Frankie and then being sick all down my beautiful dress. I am so sorry Chrissie, to bring such shame on you in front of everyone.'

'Don't be upset Heather. I think one of the boys might have put some moonshine in your punch. They wouldn't have realised how badly it would affect you. Best if you don't mention any of this to your father. We don't want to upset him.'

118

'Do you think that's what happened? Father would be so angry if he knew, so you're right, it's best he doesn't. We need all those boys to keep the farm going. But what will we tell him happened? He's bound to know we didn't come back with the boys last night.'

Just then there was a gentle knock on the door and Jeannie popped her head round when I called 'Come in.'

'Good morning Chrissie. Good morning Heather. I hope you are feeling better this morning, honey. Here's some hot water so that you can have a wash. There's some breakfast waiting for you downstairs, and Colin has arrived to take you home in the buggy. He's also brought you these clothes to change into.'

She threw a calico bag onto the bed. Although I was grateful, I wondered how Colin knew where to find our clothes.

'Thanks Jeannie. You're a good friend. We'll be down shortly.'

Colin was sitting eating a hearty breakfast of pancakes and bacon, which normally Heather and I would have enjoyed, but we both pushed our food around the plate, hardly eating or talking. I couldn't help wondering if Colin had put some moonshine in my punch, hoping to seduce me. If that was true, then he hadn't changed from the person he had been back in North Uist and he was not to be trusted. But I felt powerless to do anything about it. We were so reliant on him now.

CHAPTER THIRTY-FOUR

After the dance, Heather was quieter than normal around the boys, and she avoided Frankie as much as possible. She obviously blamed him for what had happened that night, but we did not speak of it. As time went on, I wondered if Heather was growing overly fond of Colin. Her youthful face lit up whenever she saw him, and she always gave him larger helpings of food than Frankie and the others. I wondered if I should speak to Colin, but I didn't want to embarrass Heather by letting him know she was soft on him. He was already too confident for my liking and after what happened at the Golden Sheaf, I wasn't certain he was trustworthy. I hoped Roderick would recover soon so that Colin could move on to pastures new. It would soon be spring and time for the second busiest period for the farm, so if we could just get through that, Roderick might be better in time for this year's harvest.

One day when Colin was at work, I spoke to Heather.

'I notice you and Colin seem to be getting closer, Heather. Am I right?'

'Och Chrissie,' she said in that funny half Scottish half Cree accent she had. 'I'm only showing him how I calm the horses. He says he's seen no one doing that before and wants to learn.'

'And can you teach him? I thought it was an innate sense that your mother's people had.'

'Perhaps it is, but I'm trying to teach him, anyway. I could teach you too if you wished.'

'No, no, you're fine. But I just wondered if you were soft on him. You're almost sixteen and growing into a very beautiful young woman. I've seen Frankie and the others looking at you with admiration when you serve their meals.'

'Huh, Frankie. I wouldn't go with him if he was the last man on earth after what he did.'

'So, you know for certain that it was Frankie who put alcohol in your drink?'

'Well, not for sure. But who else could it have been? It was him who gave me the punch.'

'What about Colin? The glass of punch he gave me made me feel hot and light-headed.'

'Colin wouldn't do that, Chrissie. He cares about us too much.'

'And do you care for him?'

Heather smiled and looked down, her pale russet skin growing warm.

'Don't be daft. I'm only showing him how to talk to the horses.'

'But if he were to kiss you, what would you do?'

'I would say I'm not allowed and then tell my father. He told me what Colin did to you back in Scotland, so I know I need to be careful Chrissie.'

'Roderick told you about that. When?'

'When Colin first came to the farm. He doesn't like Colin, you know. He thinks he's pretending to be nice, but I'm not so sure. I think he has changed. Don't you?'

'I hope so, for all our sakes. We are relying on him quite a lot just now and I don't want to be worrying about him letting us down.'

We talked no more on the subject as we busied ourselves preparing the food for the evening meal, but I had a bad feeling about it. As I hummed one of the old songs that my mother and I used to sing when we worked together, I felt an overwhelming longing for home and realised how much I missed my mother.

'Chrissie? What's it like to be kissed?' Heather asked in a small voice, interrupting my reverie.

I looked at her and smiled despite the knot of anxiety that cramped my stomach. Was she asking because Colin had tried to kiss her? I hoped not. I remembered the time Colin had tried to kiss me when I was walking home from work and his rough manhandling of me at the market in Lochmaddy. I also remembered his more recent attempt to kiss me and how much I was tempted. The thought of him doing that to Heather made me feel sick. But she was a young woman, and it was natural for her to be curious, so I wanted to answer her as honestly as I could. I thought of the sweet kisses that Roderick and I had shared before he became ill, and my eyes watered slightly as I realised how much I was missing my husband, even though he was only in the next room.

'Kisses can be very sweet if they are with the right person, Heather. But it's important to know that they are the forerunner of what's called intercourse when a man and a woman become one flesh. They can be very enjoyable, and they arouse changes in your body. This is all part of what happens in order that we have babies and keep humanity going, but in our culture, it's best to be married before you have a child. Life for you will be difficult enough because of your mixed heritage, so having an illegitimate child would make your life doubly difficult.'

I could see that Heather was looking worried and gave her a hug.

'I'm sorry, pet lamb, I'm scaring you. If Colin, or anyone else tries to kiss you, let me know. Men can be ruled by their urges and can sometimes behave inappropriately towards women, so we must always be on our guard. It's important not to be too flirtatious and make them think we want them to kiss us when we don't.'

'Thanks Chrissie. I think I understand what you mean.'

When we had finished our preparations, I got ready to go into town.

'I'm going into town for the Homemakers' meeting and to pick up my mail. Do you want to come with me, Heather?'

'Not today, Chrissie. I want to spend some time with Father. I think he's really bored now that he's getting better, and it's too cold yet to sit out in the sun. His bedroom is not the lightest of places so I said I would make some bright cushions and curtains to cheer him up.'

'You're a good lass. Thank you. I don't know what I would have done without you these last couple of years.'

We hugged each other warmly, and I was grateful for all that Heather had brought into my life. I would just need to keep an eye on things and make sure Colin had no opportunity to take advantage of her innocence. Little did I know it was too late.

CHAPTER THIRTY-FIVE

When I reached town, I saw that Colin's horse was outside the Golden Sheaf. My stomach filled with butterflies as I wondered why he was here rather than on our farm working as he was being paid to do. It was fortunate that the Golden Sheaf was a temperance hotel as I could remember as clear as if it were yesterday the smell of whisky on his breath that day at the market. There would be no Roderick to save me if anything bad were to happen today. His behaviour at the party and my conversation with Heather had left me suspicious of him, although I accepted I was partly to blame for what had happened at the party even if he had laced my drink with alcohol. I sighed, thinking it was so long since I'd felt desirable to anyone. Apart from a brief period of happiness when we had first arrived in Canada, things had not gone well with Roderick and now he had an illness that would leave him weak and perhaps impotent. I was still a young woman with the needs of a young woman. No wonder Colin's flirting had tempted me. When I realised where my thoughts were going, I stopped them instantly. What was I thinking? I had responsibilities. I was no longer a silly young woman thinking that I could be a Factor's wife.

When I reached the meeting, I looked for Jeannie. She was normally easy to spot because of her red curls, but today she wasn't to be seen. I wondered why and sat down beside Amelia.

'Hello Amelia. How are you today?'

'I am well, thank you, Chrissie. Yourself?'

'Yes, I'm fine. Just a bit fed up if truth be told. I feel like I have all the responsibilities of the world on my shoulders, what with having to work with the men to keep the farm going now that Roderick is ill, not to mention looking after my little Roddy.'

'Even with that handsome manager of yours working with the men now?'

'Well yes, it is helpful having him and he is good with the men. It also means I find it easier to come to these meetings.'

'Well, it's good you have managed to come along as Violet McNaughton is speaking today.'

'Is she? I've heard she's a wonderful speaker and such an inspiration for us women.'

Just then I saw Jeannie coming in and waved her over, as I had kept a seat for her. She was breathless when she sat down.

'Sorry I'm late. I thought I would never get away. There was a crowd of men in the hotel for lunch who had obviously been drinking, although where they got it from, I don't know. They were getting raucous, and Bill always gets me to help him out when that happens as he thinks my presence helps to keep the men in their place. But not today. In fact, your manager, Colin, was particularly troublesome. He was trying to get fresh with me and, of course, Bill got jealous and threw him out onto the street. I was affronted.'

'Where did he go? He should be at our farm. Who is supervising the men?'

My heart was racing, and I was full of questions.

'Try to stay calm, Chrissie. I don't know where he went, but I don't think you'll get much sense out of him today. Try to relax and listen to Mrs McNaughton.'

As Mrs McNaughton began talking, for the first time in my life, I felt myself admiring a woman. I had seen no one talk with such intelligence and enthusiasm and despite her 4'10 height, she was extremely elegant and persuasive. She was not against the Homemakers, but she wanted more for women. She believed that men and women had to co-operate together to make a living, but they needed to live a life as well and it was important that women should have free time from their chores to discover their higher selves. I was so caught up in her talk, it was time to leave before I knew it. Saying goodbye to my friends, I left the meeting thinking of all that Mrs McNaughton had said and how I might find my higher self, so the last thing on my mind was Colin Donaldson.

My heart sank when I saw him hanging about where my horse was tied up. As Jeannie had said, he looked the worse for wear. His clothes were dirty, and he had a scrape on his face where he had obviously landed in the dirt outside the hotel. I took a deep breath.

'Good afternoon Colin. I hear you've had a bit of trouble in the hotel today.'

He looked up at me and tears fell from his eyes.

'What is it Colin?' I said, going over and taking his hands, forgetting my mistrust of him. 'Has something happened?'

'Yes. It's Victoria. I got a letter today from my father to say that she was seriously ill again with the polio and might die.'

'Oh no. Victoria. Lovely Victoria. No wonder you are upset, Colin. Come here, come here,' I said, putting my arms around him and patting him on the back like a child.

Unfortunately, Colin didn't respond like a child and before I knew what was happening, his lips were on mine and he was kissing me. I could taste the sour/sweet taste of something on his breath and it reminded me of that day on North Uist. Anger rose in me, and I pushed him away, causing him to fall on the ground. I thought he looked ridiculous lying there and wondered how I could ever have thought him handsome. He was a drunken philanderer and now a sobbing one.

'I can't bear that my little sister is dying. I can't bear it,' he howled.

Just at that, Jeannie and Amelia came along.

'What's wrong? What's going on here? Are you alright Chrissie?'

It was Jeannie's turn to be full of questions.

'I'm fine,' I told them, deciding it was best not to say that Colin had tried to kiss me. The fewer people who knew about that, the better if he was to continue to work at the farm. 'It's Colin. He's just heard that his little sister is dying. She had the polio, and it has come back, but it looks like it will claim her life this time. She's only the same age as me.'

'Oh, that's so sad.'

'He's in no fit state to go back to work, Jeannie. Can you let him have a room to sleep it off?'

'Yes, of course. I'll get Bill to give me a hand to get him up and into the hotel.'

'When Colin sobers up, ask him to report to me at the farm.'

'Will do'.

CHAPTER THIRTY-SIX

When I returned home, I went to see how Roderick was doing. Of course, he asked me how my meeting had gone and as I told him about Mrs McNaughton and what a wonderful speaker she was, he smiled widely. I realised I sounded like him when he was telling me what it felt like to till virgin ground when he first arrived in Canada.

'Is my wife becoming a suffragette now?' he laughed.

'And what if I was?' I said, smiling at this man that I loved so much. I decided I better tell Roderick about meeting Colin.

'I bumped into Colin when I was in town.'

Roderick frowned. Any mention of Colin always riled him up.

'He wasn't at work because he had bad news from home and wasn't up to it.'

'What kind of news?'

'Victoria, his sister, is dying from a second bout of the polio.'

'Oh, I'm sorry Chrissie. You must be upset. Didn't you used to work with her?'

'I did and I am so sad to hear about her, but it surprised me at how upset Colin was. He was drunk and crying.'

'I hope he tried nothing on with you. I've never trusted that man.'

'Don't be daft Roderick. He was too drunk to try anything on with anyone. I could have knocked him down with one light push. I wouldn't have needed a knight in shining armour like you to save me.'

I realised I was feeling quite proud of myself as I thought about how I had pushed Colin onto the ground. Mrs McNaughton's talk had definitely had a positive effect on me. I took Roderick's hand and smiled at him, trying to lighten his mood.

'How are you feeling, my love? I can't wait until you're back in bed with me and perhaps we could make another little baby together.'

'I long for nothing else, but you'd be better off without me. You deserve someone your own age who's fit and healthy, not an old man like me.'

'Ach you're not old, you're just mature. There's no one else for me, Roderick. No one.' And I meant it. Roderick was the only man for me, and I thanked God silently that He had kept me from temptation, and I could still call myself a loyal wife.

The men came in for their dinner not long after and the house was pandemonium for a while. They were all in high spirits and I wondered if they had got hold of some of the moonshine that Colin had been drinking, but I couldn't smell anything. Perhaps it was just that Spring was in the air.

'Where was Colin today?' Frankie asked. 'He didn't come and give us our usual instructions.'

'Lucky for me then that you know what you're doing,' I smiled, trying to divert them from why Colin wasn't there today. I hoped he would be back on duty the next day, but if Victoria was dying, he might want to go home and then what would we do.

When the men had gone back to their quarters, I turned the light out and sat at the fire thinking about the day's events. Colin's kiss, my reaction and Mrs McNaughton's talk had certainly stirred me up and I wondered if what I had told Roderick was true. While he was alive, he would be the only one for me, but what would I do if he died and I was left on my own, a widow with a young son to raise? Would I try to find another husband? All my life I had thought that women needed a man at their side, but if what Mrs McNaughton said was true, that wasn't so. While it might be nice to be married to a man who loved me and to have children, times were changing, and I no longer felt I needed to be married to be secure. Hadn't I proved that since Roderick had become ill? I thought about my Aunt Katie, who had chosen not to be married and to live her life as a single woman. If she could do it, so could I if I needed to. Why not?

Heather came in with some wood for the fire and looked over at me curiously.

129

'You're looking dreamy, Chrissie. What are you thinking?'

'About the future. I'm hoping that Roderick will be back on his feet soon, but I know he will never be the same. He will never be the man that I married and I'm trying to figure out what kind of life we could have.'

'Do you think you could keep the farm on if Father wasn't able to work on it?'

'I don't know Heather.'

'Perhaps Colin could stay here with us permanently and help father to run the farm.'

'I saw Colin in town today.'

'Colin? Why wasn't he at work. I wondered why I hadn't seen him today.'

'He was drunk. He'd had bad news from home and was very distressed. His sister Victoria is seriously ill and dying. I don't know what he'll do now. Perhaps he'll go home as his mother and father will be devastated to lose Victoria and will need his support.'

'Oh, poor Colin. That is so hard. Being so far away from home at a time like this.'

'I'm wondering if we should go home too, Heather. I don't believe your father will ever be able to run the farm again, and I don't know that I want to. It's been a hard nine months since Roderick got ill.'

'What would happen to me if you went home?' she asked, her eyes misting up with tears.

'You would come with us, you silly girl. You're part of our family. You know that.'

'But what would people say about me. I'm a half-breed. It would disgrace father.'

I looked at Heather and knew what she said to be true, but we would need to find a way round it that would not bring shame upon us. I would need to get my thinking cap on.

'There's no need to worry about that now, Heather. If we decide to go home, it won't be for a long time.'

But it was to be sooner than I had expected.

CHAPTER THIRTY-SEVEN

Colin went home to support his family, and the place seemed quiet without him supervising the men, coming in for his meals and learning how to horse whisper. Fortunately, Roderick continued to improve and could tell Frankie what to do around the farm during spring, when the ground needed to be cultivated and seed sown. I also understood more about the workings of the farm from my conversations with Colin, so was more knowledgeable about what should happen, so we managed fine without Colin. However, when I put to Roderick the notion of going home, he was remarkably receptive to the idea.

'We'll make a bit of money from the farm Chrissie, so perhaps we could buy a shop when we go home rather than renting a croft. Would you like to do something like that?'

'I would love it Roderick. Shopkeepers get to know everything that's going on in the island.'

'I never thought you were so nosy.'

'Just natural curiosity my love.'

'What about Heather?' he said, his face turning sad. 'We wouldn't be able to take her with us. She wouldn't fit in.'

'Why wouldn't she?'

'She's a half-breed, and she has inherited more from her mother's ancestry than from her father's. She would be too different.'

'We could make up a story that would make it acceptable for her to be living with us. I told Colin she was our ward, so we could say that. He would have told people when he went home that we had her, so it would look funny if she wasn't with us.'

'But what story could we make up about how she came to be our ward?'

'Why not the same one that you told me. That her mother worked for you and died in childbirth.'

'But how did her mother get pregnant? It wouldn't work. Everyone would think I was her father.'

'Perhaps. Her eyes are very blue, just like yours.'

Roderick looked uncomfortable, no doubt worrying that I would become jealous again. My cheeks grew pink when I thought about how I had been. What a difference two years and a baby make.

'Well let's put our heads together. I think we could make up a suitable story if we tried hard enough. But I'm telling you something Roderick, we are not leaving her behind.'

He took my face in his hands just the way he had done on our wedding night.

'I know why I love you so much, Chrissie. You are such a lovely person. Thank you.'

As time went on, I could see that Heather was pining. She must have been a little in love with Colin, but there was no way there could ever have been a match between them, just as there was no way there could ever have been a match between him and me. Although I was of the same race, I was not of the same background or status; poor Heather wasn't even of the same race. Heather became peakier and although I didn't like to think she was pining for Colin, I preferred it to thinking she had caught the consumption. How would I cope if both Heather and Roderick were ill, although she seemed to be putting weight on rather than losing it the way Roderick had? Then it dawned on me. She was pregnant. But how, with whom? It must be one of the hands. Maybe she had forgiven Frankie, and they had become a couple. I had seen him looking at her sometimes. I needed to think through how to approach Heather, as I didn't want to jump right in and frighten her out of her wits. She was more likely to confide in me if I broached the subject more subtly.

'Morning Heather,' I smiled at her the next morning. 'How are you today? I must say you've been looking peaky lately and I'm wondering if we should get the doctor in to have a look at you. What do you think?'

'Please don't Chrissie.'

'Why not? You are unwell, aren't you? What if you have tuberculosis like Roderick?'

132

Heather bit her lip.

'I think I'm having a baby. I haven't wanted to admit it in case you throw me out. I will bring disgrace to you and just when you were thinking of us all going back to Scotland together.

Tears flowed from her eyes.

'Who is the father, Heather? Is there any chance that you might marry your sweetheart?'

Heather began to sob and shook her head vigorously.

'No Chrissie. It was Colin. I told him I thought I was pregnant, and it was not long after I gave him my news that he told you his sister was dying, and he needed to go home. He obviously wanted nothing to do with me.'

I felt myself growing hot with rage. What a scoundrel. Taking advantage of a young girl like that. He hadn't changed at all. All that sweet talk and helping had all been a façade. He was still a villain, and it made me wonder if Victoria was even dying. I would need to write to my mother to find out. I resisted the temptation to rant and rave at Heather for being so stupid, but hadn't I only resisted his advances back in North Uist because I didn't want a visit from the minister. I would need to talk to Roderick and decide what to do. I felt sick. Why did everything have to go wrong? Where are you, God? You just give me one disaster after another to cope with. I can't bear it. To my surprise, I burst into tears, and it was Heather who ended up trying to comfort me.

CHAPTER THIRTY-EIGHT

'I'll go away. I'll go to the reservation. I think my mother's brother still lives there. He might take me in.'

'I don't see how he would take you in when your poor mother had to leave the reservation when her father died. Those bureaucrats who drew up that Indian Bill have a lot to answer for. It's left women so dependent on the men of the tribe.'

'But isn't that the same as in your culture? Aren't you dependent on Father? They were only bringing us into line with what you do in Scotland. Don't you agree with it?'

I thought back to the conversation with my mother before all this sorry business with Roderick had happened and wondered how I could have been so naïve as to think it was alright for my husband to look after me and that it wasn't important for me to have the vote. Well, life had taught me a lesson. Men were undependable. Even poor Roderick had let me down, albeit because he was sick, not because he was bad, but it had still left me vulnerable. Having the support of the Homemakers' Club and the Women's Grain Grower's Society had saved me. Other women had helped me, not men. They had only tried to expose my weaknesses and take advantage, just like Colin had done with Heather. But I needed to calm down. I needed to think about how I would break this news to Roderick. Now that he was getting better, I didn't want him to have a relapse.

'You're right Heather, but since I've moved to this godforsaken country, I've changed my mind about that. Don't even think about going to the reservation. You are part of our family, and we will do whatever it takes.'

'You are being very kind. I thought you would be so angry with me Chrissie. You do have a bit of a temper sometimes.'

'I know and I'm sorry I made you feel like that.'

I paused before going on to my next question. How had it happened? When did it happen? I hoped to God that Colin hadn't forced himself on her.

134

'How did it happen? Did he hurt you?'

'No. He said he loved me and wanted to marry me but that you and Father would object, so I had to keep it secret. We met when you went to your meetings in town and sometimes, he came into my room during the night.'

I was stunned. How could this have happened to Heather under our own roof? Roderick would be outraged.

'You must be heartbroken that he has gone. I'm so sorry.'

'Perhaps we'll meet him when we get back to Scotland and we can be married then.'

'Perhaps, but I wouldn't get my hopes up, Heather. I think Colin's actions have shown his intentions towards you. I'll need to speak with your father. Do you want to be there when I speak to him, or do you want me to talk to him on my own?'

'I would prefer that you spoke to him. I can't bear to see the disappointment in his eyes.'

Disappointment was the least of it. Roderick was livid.

'That man, that bastard. I knew he wasn't to be trusted. You are too naïve, Chrissie inviting that man to work here. And now look what's happened. That's Heather's life ruined. I thought we could take her to Scotland, and she could have a fresh start, even find a husband, but now. There is no hope of that ever happening.'

His voice was shaking with rage, and he struck the nearest thing to him with his walking stick. The commode shook with the force of the blow, making some of its contents spill out on to the floor. Just as well Colin wasn't here. He would have been a dead man if that stick had landed on his head with such force. The smell of urine was disgusting, but it stopped Roderick in his tracks. He realised it would need to be cleaned up and that it would be me who would do the cleaning, so it cooled him down.

'I'm sorry Chrissie. I know it's not your fault. It's mine for getting this damned illness. It left us all vulnerable to any scoundrel who came along offering to help.'

Suddenly, he began coughing and seemed to have trouble catching his breath. A bluish tinge came over his face, and his

135

chest was heaving up and down. I was terrified he was going to die. I hoped he wouldn't have a relapse as he had been doing so well. It took a while, but gradually his colour returned to normal, and the coughing subsided.

'Where is Colin now?' he gasped. 'I might get the Mounties onto him.'

'I don't know. I'm assuming he's back in Scotland. He was very distressed the last time I saw him.'

'I bet he was. Running away like the coward he is and leaving a young girl to fend for herself.'

He coughed again, but less severely this time.

'I'm a bloody useless excuse for a man. Leave me be Chrissie. I want to be on my own to think about what to do.'

CHAPTER THIRTY-NINE

The next day, Roderick told me what he had decided. We would wait until Heather had the baby and then go home. We would register the baby as belonging to us so that when we went back to Scotland, everyone would think Heather's baby was ours and she would not carry the stigma of being an unmarried mother. We would write to our respective families, telling them I was with child again and that after the baby was born, we would return to Scotland. The reason we would give, which was true, was that the tuberculosis had incapacitated Roderick and he could no longer manage the farm.

'It is the only way to do it if Heather is not to be ruined,' Roderick said.

'Do you think it will work? Won't people wonder how we could have made a baby when you have been so ill? The baby might also look different from us. Heather's skin is much darker than ours. How would we explain it? '

'I don't know. Maybe we are best not writing to our families until after the baby is born and we see what it looks like.'

'Also, don't you think you better ask Heather what she wants before we write home?'

'Heather will do as I tell her. She has acted foolishly, and I am extremely disappointed in her. As to the other thing, why don't we sleep together tonight and get our marriage back on a proper footing. I think you'll find I am more than able to make a baby if we were to choose to do so.'

I hesitated, thinking of the coughing fit he had had earlier, and realised I wasn't quite ready to get into bed with him yet.

'I'm not sure that's a good idea. What if I got pregnant? We couldn't pretend that Heather's baby was ours too.'

'Yes, I can see that it would be a problem. But I am lonely Chrissie. I want to cuddle up with you again. The doctor has said I'm not infectious.'

137

'Well, let's leave it for another month just to be on the safe side. And let's talk to Heather. I know you are her father, but it would be courteous to include her in our discussions about her baby.'

I felt uneasy. I didn't like the way Roderick was deciding about Heather, as if she had no rights. No woman should have her child taken from her without her permission. Even though she would still live with us and would see her child every day, she could never hear them call her mama. She would have to spend her life pretending that she was their sister and watch another woman love and care for her child. It would be so hard for her.

'Alright Chrissie. Get Heather in here and I'll let her know what I've decided.'

'Perhaps it would be better to say that this is what you are suggesting should happen rather than telling her it's what you've decided.'

'She doesn't have a choice, Chrissie. I'm sorry.'

When Heather came into the room, she lowered her eyes, frightened to look at Roderick.

'Don't be afraid, Heather. I will not shout at you, but I have to say that I think you have been a very foolish girl getting into trouble like this, especially with that immoral ruffian. I am extremely disappointed that you would do such a thing.'

'I know, Father,' she said, tears streaming from her eyes. 'I'm so sorry. You warned me, but I didn't heed your warning. Please forgive me.'

Heather knelt in front of her father, looking up at him beseechingly. I hoped Roderick wasn't infectious, as the doctor had said, as Heather was kneeling far too close to him for my liking.

'I forgive you, Heather,' Roderick said, giving her a pat on the head. 'Now get up. Chrissie and I have something to discuss with you.'

He nodded over at me, inviting me to begin.

'Come and sit beside me, Heather,' I said, patting the chair next to the one I was sitting in. 'Your father and I have been discussing what to do for the best and we've come up with an idea that we would like you to consider.'

Heather came over, wiping her eyes and nose with one of Roderick's unused handkerchiefs, and sat beside me, looking at me expectantly.

'We wondered how you would feel if, instead of you registering your child, Roderick and I do it. We would register ourselves as your baby's parents and as we are going back to Scotland, no one would know that you had been pregnant. This will allow you to keep your reputation, which means it will be easier for you to find a suitable husband.'

Heather was silent, and I wondered what she was thinking. Sometimes she was quite inscrutable.

'So, you would be my baby's mother Chrissie and I would be their sister.'

'Yes.'

'But what if Colin wants to marry me when we get back to Scotland? When he sees his child, surely he will want to do the right thing for the sake of his child if not for me.'

'Have you learned nothing, Heather? That man is an unscrupulous villain. He will never do the right thing. The right thing would have been to not seduce you in the first place. You need to see Colin Donaldson for what he is,' replied Roderick, becoming red in the face with indignation.

'But I want to write to him, Father, and ask him. Surely you would allow me to do that. We have another six months before my baby is due. That will allow plenty of time for me to contact Colin and see what he has to say.'

Roderick coughed, and Chrissie decided it would be best to leave their discussion for another day. As Heather said, they had another six months before any firm decision would need to be made.

The next day, however, a letter arrived from Victoria sending her usual letter and magazines, which changed everything as far as Heather was concerned. In her letter Victoria mentioned nothing about being ill again and in fact she told us she had gone to Bath in England to take the waters for her legs, and she felt it had helped her. She even asked after Colin, so it was clear he had lied about her illness and had not gone home to Scotland. Naturally, Heather was distressed that he had lied to her but that he could have lied like that about his sister shocked her.

'What kind of man is he to do that, Chrissie? I'm glad he didn't want to marry me. I would not have wished to be tied to a man like that.'

'Well said Heather. You are better off without him. But you know it's alright to be sad too. You've had an enormous disappointment.'

Her eyes welled up, but she brushed the tears away.

'I have made a huge mistake, and it's one I won't make again. I am finished with men forever. I will tell Father that I agree with his suggestion, but I want to get a job when we move to Scotland. Although you will tell everyone that my baby is yours, we will know that it is mine and I want to support it as much as I can. I can't leave it all to you and Father. You are already doing much more than I deserve.'

She then broke into heart-rending sobs, and it took me a long time to soothe her. Poor Heather. She was heartbroken and at such a tender age. How would she ever recover from this? I cursed Colin Donaldson for his selfish actions and prayed to God to punish him.

CHAPTER FORTY

Little Donald Ewen Macdonald was born on 1 December 1913. Although the runner tracks through the snow had been made, which normally made travel in the winter easier, there had been a ferocious windstorm. This had resulted in the soft snow that sat precariously on the side of the tracks being blown into them and making travel difficult. When Dr Munro phoned to tell us he couldn't get through, Heather and I weren't too worried.

'We'll do this together, Heather. You are a brilliant lassie where delivering babies is concerned,'

Heather laughed.

'Aye, other people's Chrissie. We'll see how it goes with this one.'

That all changed when we realised the baby was not lying in the correct birthing position. No matter how much I tried to massage the baby round as Heather instructed me to do, it remained in the same position.

'You might have to cut me, Chrissie,' Heather said, between contractions. 'Best telephone the doctor and ask him what you should do.'

I couldn't help but admire Heather's calmness, as I was panicking. I had never delivered a baby before and the only thing I knew about it was when I had Roddy and his birth had been straightforward, with no complications. Also, Heather was becoming tired, as she had been in labour for a long time now.

Roderick had taken Roddy over to the shanty so that he would not be frightened if Heather screamed during the delivery, so I pulled on my coat and ran over. I was going to need help. I banged on the door, shouting for Roderick. When he opened the door, I glimpsed the warm cosiness within and wished with all my heart that I didn't need to shatter it.

'Roderick, we need to telephone the doctor. The baby is in the wrong position for birthing, and I've tried everything that Heather

141

had told me, but it is making no difference. Oh, Roderick I'm so scared.'

'Hush, hush. Everything will be alright.'

Turning into the cabin, he called to the lads that he was going over to the house and would they mind Roddy. I glimpsed their worried faces through the gap, then ran back to Heather. Roderick telephoned the doctor and told him what was happening, although Heather's excruciating screams told him the extent of her pain more than anything Roderick could describe. She looked so young and vulnerable lying in such agony and I wished I could take her pain from her.

Eventually, it was all over. Under the doctor's instructions, I made a cut to help remove the baby. Heather lost a lot of blood despite my best efforts and was extremely weak when I placed her son in her arms. He was a healthy boy and cried with the freshness of new life. She looked at him for a long time, then smiled up at Roderick and me.

'He is beautiful, and I think he looks a lot like you, Father. Even his hair is auburn like yours. I think you will be able to carry out this deception upon which you have decided, but I do not think that I shall ever see Scotland.'

'Don't talk like that Heather, you will be with us and your son,' I said, tears pouring from my eyes.

'You forget, Chrissie, that I have seen a lot of births and deaths. Thank you, for what you are doing for me. I know you will be a wonderful mother to my son.'

Roderick was sobbing quietly and didn't try to persuade Heather that she was going to live.

'What shall we call this boy of yours, Heather?' he asked.

'Call him Donald so that he has part of his father's name. I hope he will be a better man than he is.'

She lay for a little while, cradling her son before speaking again.

'Father, would you take a photograph of me with Donald on that camera that you bought last year? I would like to think that one day he might know the truth about his birth and that it would bring him comfort to know what I looked like.'

So that is what we did. Roderick fetched the Brownie, and I put some rouge on Heather's lips and cheeks, then brushed her hair in preparation for having her photograph taken with her son. It was a tradition in those times to have a *memento mori* by a professional photographer of the deceased, but we were doing it while she was still alive and able to hold her son in her arms. When it was done, Heather again spoke.

'Thank you for being my father. Thank you for taking care of my mother and me. If you are my father, I couldn't have better blood in me and if not, I couldn't have had a more loving upbringing than you gave me. I know that my little boy will be safe with you. I'm sorry that you had to see me like this. It is not right for a father to see his daughter having a baby.'

Roderick kissed her tenderly on the forehead.

'You were wonderful, Heather. I wouldn't have missed it for the world. Now give me that beautiful boy of yours and you get some sleep.'

We knew Heather wouldn't last the night, so Roderick and I took it in turns to sit with her, burning the herbs that she told us to, which was the Cree tradition to accompany the dying on their journey into the next world. The boys came over to pay their respects, but it was Frankie who lingered longest, holding her hand and whispering to her with tears falling from his eyes. How I wished Heather had fallen for Frankie rather than Colin. She would have her whole life ahead of her instead of lying on her deathbed at the tender age of sixteen. The sadness of it all overwhelmed me, and I knew that life would never be the same. I was sitting with baby Donald in my arms, singing a Gaelic lullaby when Heather finally drew her last breath. Roderick and I knelt and prayed that God would take her safely to Him.

143

CHAPTER FORTY-ONE

There was nothing left for the doctor to do when he arrived the next day except issue a certificate of death. When he asked for Heather's birth certificate so that he could record her name, date of birth and the names of her parents properly, Roderick hesitated. Heather's birth had never been registered. Because of the killing of Jim Adams, he and Lily had decided not to register Heather in case the Mounties would get wind of it and come looking for Lily. Roderick looked over at me and took a deep breath before speaking.

'Her full name is Heather Waskatamwi Macdonald. Her mother was Waskatamwi Macdonald, and her father is me, Roderick Macdonald.'

I nodded over to Roderick and smiled my silent consent to his decision to acknowledge Heather as his daughter. The doctor glanced at Roderick, then wrote out the certificate without further comment.

The matter of little Donald's birth certificate was more problematic. Dr Munro was very understanding when Roderick explained Heather had agreed that the baby should be raised as our son, but he hummed and hawed at giving out a false birth certificate to that effect.

'I understand why you want the little boy's birth certificate to have your names on it. He would have a better chance in life if he was seen to be of legitimate birth with Scottish parents, but I could be struck off if the authorities found out I had falsified information.'

'But no one would know. We wouldn't tell anyone what you had done and as we are going back to Scotland, no one in Saskatchewan will be any the wiser.'

He got up from the chair he was sitting in and began pacing the room. I realised I was holding my breath as I let out a loud sigh when he sat down at the table again and spoke.

'I have an idea, which you can take or leave.'

'What is it?' asked Roderick.

144

'I will issue his birth certificate with Heather and his father's name, if you know who that is, but I will also give you a blank form which if you choose to falsify the details will make you responsible for breaking the law rather than me.'

Roderick and I looked at each other, then nodded at Dr Munro.

'We'll take it,' said Roderick.

'You know you will have to register Heather's death and Donald's birth in Yorkton? If you feel it will look suspicious registering a birth and a death at the same time, you don't need to register this little lad straight away. Sometimes, in the winter, it's months before children are registered.'

So that was how little Donald ended up with two birth certificates. The doctor completed the legal one, naming Heather Macdonald as the mother and Colin Donaldson as the father with the words 'not admitted' in brackets and Roderick wrote out the false certificate putting us as the parents. We never registered Donald's birth in Canada, deciding to wait until we were home so that no awkward questions would be asked.

On the day we buried Heather, I again cursed Colin Donaldson for his selfishness and prayed to God to make something bad happen to him, too. We held a small gathering in our homestead to allow people to pay their respects to a much-loved member of our community. I put Heather's best dress on her and rubbed a little rouge on her cheeks and lips. As people mingled around the casket while chatting, eating, and drinking, they commented on how beautiful she looked. Everyone cried at the loss of such a young life and encouraged Roderick to have a *memento mori* by a professional photographer, as was the custom. We didn't tell them we had already taken a photograph of her while she was still alive.

We buried Heather beside her mother in a cemetery on the outskirts of town, so at least she wouldn't be alone when we went back to Scotland. I was wracked with grief and guilt at how I had treated Heather when I first arrived in Canada. Even more so that I had allowed Colin into our lives. I should have trusted my instinct

145

and never let him through the door or sacked him when I suspected him of lacing mine and Heather's drink. Then none of this would have happened.

Roderick was bereft. Although he didn't know for certain that Heather was his daughter, he loved her as if she were. I hoped he would receive comfort from little Donald, but it didn't work out that way. It was as if every time he looked at Donald, it set his grief and rage against Colin in motion again. He even seemed jealous when I fed the baby with the bottle I had from when Roddy was being weaned. I only wished I could feed him from my breast as it was much safer and more wholesome, but I consoled myself that the formula that was available now was much improved. But it was a very difficult few months waiting for the farm to be sold and booking our passage back to Scotland. I couldn't wait to get home to the safety of North Uist, where I would have the support of my friends and family, and get away from this hostile, inhospitable land.

CHAPTER FORTY-TWO

Roderick sold the farm to another farmer that he knew, a Ukrainian who was doing well and wanted to extend his land holding. The sale was easy because of the way the government had originally set up the homesteads. They had used a grid system and boundaries were therefore easy to distinguish and the legal paperwork was straightforward. Jake and Hamish stayed on, but Frankie left. He had taken Heather's death badly. Packing up was hard as Roderick couldn't help much and with two babies to look after, it wasn't a simple task. Amelia and Jeannie helped as much as they could and, at last, all was ready to go. My heart was heavy as I thought about leaving Heather behind, but maybe it was for the best. She was here in her own land where her mother's ancestors had lived. I looked at Donald and wondered what kind of life he would have in Scotland. Although it had been several months, Roderick was still disinterested in Donald. It would not be easy convincing people he was our baby if he didn't change his attitude towards him.

We left Canada in June 1914, just over four years from when we had arrived there from Scotland. I found it hard to believe that so much had happened in that short period, and none of it good. I had no regrets about leaving Canada, although I would miss Amelia and Jeannie. As we waited amid the hustle and bustle of the quay in Montreal to board the ship that would take us home, my thoughts went back to our wait at the quay in Glasgow and the mixed feelings I'd had about my husband and moving to Canada. I hardly knew Roderick back then and as I looked at him now, his body emaciated by his illness and his features set in a grim mask by grief, I wondered if I knew him now.

The ship's horn blew, and we silently boarded the ship together with the other passengers. I was delighted that Roderick had let me persuade him to buy second-class tickets for our journey home. The thought of travelling in steerage with two small children was unbearable. Normally, he was careful with his money, but his

147

grief at Heather's death and the aftermath of his illness had left him with little fight in him, so I had persuaded him easily. What a difference from our journey over to Canada. We had a cabin with a proper bed and cots for the boys. Waiters served good quality tasty food in the dining room, while we sat at tables with white tablecloths and silver cutlery. I felt sorry for those in steerage and sometimes saved bread and fruit from our supplies to give out to those below.

The sea was much calmer too, so I wasn't sick at all, and I found myself enjoying the voyage. It was good not to have to cook and clean and do all the other things I had to do on the homestead. I knew once we got home my life would again become one of work and responsibility, so I decided to enjoy this brief interlude as much as I could. The more I relaxed, the more agitated Roderick became. He was short with me and grumpy about the children when they cried or misbehaved. He spent most of his time up on deck and left me to my own devices with the babies, and I have to admit I was glad.

One night, halfway through the journey, Donald would not stop crying. He was feverish and appeared to be in pain.

'Can't you stop that damned child from crying, Chrissie. I'm trying to get some sleep here.'

'He's not well, Roderick. I think we should fetch the doctor. Will you go?'

'Are you sure he's not just getting his teeth through?'

'I don't know, but he is boiling up and is coughing. I'm worried he's caught the consumption.'

Roderick's face paled.

'Let me look at him.'

After he had examined Donald, he turned to me.

'I don't think it's consumption, but I'll fetch the doctor, anyway.'

I was sobbing quietly. I couldn't bear for something to happen to Heather's son. It would be too much. For the first time since Heather died, Roderick's face was soft, and he took me in his arms.

148

'Don't worry mo *ghraidh*, God will keep him safe. I won't be long.'

The doctor arrived shortly thereafter and, on examining Donald, reassured us he didn't have the consumption.

'Your little boy has a fever, but nothing to worry about. I believe he is teething, which can sometimes cause high temperatures. Just keep him comfortable and make sure he drinks plenty. I will give you some medicine to help him sleep.'

'Thank you, doctor, so much,' I said, wiping my tears away. 'Our daughter died when we were in Canada, and we couldn't bear to lose this little one as well.'

The doctor nodded sympathetically, but death was not unusual in his line of business. I wondered what it was like to face death every day and be powerless to prevent it. There seemed so many diseases that could steal human life, and ships were notorious breeding grounds for some of them, especially when travelling in steerage in such close contact with others.

When the doctor left, Roderick cried softly for a long time, cradling the baby in his arms.

'I'm so sorry for how I've been to you and the little ones over the last few months, Chrissie. I've been so angry at Colin Donaldson, and I think I blamed you for allowing him into our lives.'

'You're right Roderick. I am to blame. I was so desperate to get someone to help run the farm, I didn't trust my instinct. I knew what he was like, but I ignored it. Please forgive me.'

'I forgive you and I hope you will forgive me. I have taken my rage and grief out on you and the boys, but I promise I will change. We have both made mistakes, my pet, but if we love and trust one another, we can make things right between us.'

For the first time in a long time, Roderick and I slept together, wrapped in each other's arms.

The rest of the trip home was uneventful. Donald recovered after a few days and it delighted me to see Roderick taking more of an interest in the baby, who cooed and smiled up at him. I had been worried that Roddy might be jealous. He was still a baby

149

himself and I knew children could feel upset when their parents had another child to share their affections. I remembered how I had felt when my brother Johnny had been born when I was only three. I could still remember that sinking feeling when I saw him suckling on my mother's breast. I had to be the big girl who helped when all I wanted to do was sit on my mother's lap for a cuddle. I had always made a fuss of Roddy and involved him when I was feeding Donald and I was grateful that he seemed to love his little brother. He often sat with Roderick when he was holding the baby, stroking his head, and smiling up at his father so I hoped he was not feeling jealous of Roderick's new affection for Donald.

There was great excitement as the ship berthed at Liverpool. We had a few hours before it would head up to Glasgow, so we left the ship to stretch our legs. It felt strange walking along the quay. My sea legs took a while to adjust to dry land, and I felt wobbly as we walked through the heaving mass of bodies, horses and carts carrying goods and luggage. There were all kinds of vendors on the quay trying to sell their wares to the passengers who were getting on and off the ship, but one had a large group round him, trying to buy what he offered.

'*Heir to the Austrian throne and his wife shot! Archduke killed in Sarajevo!*' shouted the boy, holding up the Liverpool Echo.

'Why is that boy making such a fuss?' I asked Roderick. 'What's so important about this Archduke?'

Roderick joined the queue and bought a paper. He scanned it quickly.

'What is it Roderick?'

'A Serbian has assassinated the heir to the Austrian throne, and it might mean war. That part of Europe has always been a difficult region and this killing will make things worse.'

'But would Scotland be involved in this war?'

'No, I don't see Great Britain becoming caught up in a war in eastern Europe, but time will tell.'

I felt uneasy. What if war broke out, and the British became involved? What would that mean for us and how would it affect our

150

new lives in North Uist? I took hold of Roderick's hand and squeezed it, seeking comfort rather than giving it. He smiled at me reassuringly.

'Don't worry, even if there is a war, our boys are too young yet to be called on to fight and I doubt whether they would want a recovering tuberculosis patient in the army.'

That brought me some comfort, but now that we were nearing home, my thoughts were turning to the practicalities of moving back to North Uist. Where would we live and what kind of work would Roderick be able to do to support us? We had a good lump sum from the sale of the farm and Roderick was of a mind to buy a shop, but I worried that there might be none available for us to buy and if there was a war what effect would that have on running such a business. I sighed and decided to put these thoughts aside and just enjoy the rest of the journey with Roderick by my side. I thanked God that he appeared to have turned a corner. I knew he would never forget Heather and wouldn't want to, but he appeared ready to look forward to the future. He was back to the Roderick I remembered at the start of our marriage, the man who loved me and whom I would love forever.

WAR AND PEACE

North Uist, 1914

CHAPTER FORTY-THREE

It was approaching the end of 1914 when I saw Colin Donaldson again. Mr Asquith had declared war on 4th August of that year just two months after we had returned home and as a result, we found ourselves living and working in the post office in Lochmaddy. The former postmaster had joined the war effort, and it left a vacancy which Roderick and I applied for. The tuberculosis had weakened Roderick so much that he was not fit enough to join the army nor to work on the croft, so this was an ideal solution for us. Roderick and I had debated whether only he should apply for the job but I wanted to work and felt it might prove too much for him to do on his own.

Women all over the country were filling the posts that were traditionally male jobs, such as driving buses and working in factories, so I saw no reason the post office would not welcome a woman into the role of joint postmistress. Women had worked for the post office in several roles for years. Roderick argued against it at first, saying that it was my role to look after the children, but I argued back that I could do both with the help of Morag working part time to help me and, in the end, he agreed. Morag was delighted with the suggestion, which would give her more money to spend. She worked as a chambermaid in the Lochmaddy Hotel in the mornings and could fit in looking after the children with her job there.

I dealt with customers wishing to buy stamps, post mail or buy postal orders, while Roderick dealt with sorting the mail and taking telegraph messages. We both took turns of delivering the mail and telegrams to the islanders who didn't pick their mail up themselves. The post office had issued us with bicycles and although it took me a while to find my balance and ride it with ease, it made delivering the mail much easier but I often thought of Clover and how much easier getting around the island would have been with my trusty friend. If I had been able to bring her with me, I wouldn't have needed to learn to ride a bicycle.

That day I was behind the counter and Colin Donaldson was the last person I was expecting to see and for a moment I didn't recognise him as he had a little moustache brushing against his upper lip and was dressed in the kilt and a uniform I didn't recognise. He looked extremely dashing as befits an officer in the army. However, my heart hardened when I recognised him and remembered all that he had done to Heather.

'Good morning, Chrissie. Victoria told me you and Roderick were working in the post office now. What made you come back from Canada?'

'It's a long story Colin and not one I care to share with you.'

'Oh well if that's how you feel. I just wondered why Heather wasn't here with you. When Victoria didn't mention a half-breed girl living with you, which would have been the talk of the island, I wondered what had become of her.'

I looked at him and wondered what to say. I wanted to shout at him not to call Heather a half-breed, to berate him for lying to me about Victoria and to tell him that Heather had died because of him, but I knew I had to tread carefully. I didn't want to ruin all our plans and make it known that Donald was a bastard. There was no way I was going to do that to him.

'Heather died.'

Colin's face became grave as he took in this news. Perhaps he had felt something for her after all.

'How?'

I hesitated. This is where I would need to tell an outright lie.

'She caught the consumption and unlike Roderick she wasn't able to fight it.'

I thought by saying this he would think that the baby had died with Heather so would not suspect that Donald was his son. It surprised me to see tears in his eyes, which he quickly covered up by pulling out a handkerchief and blowing his nose.

'My condolences on your loss. She was a lovely girl. I was very fond of her.'

155

Not fond enough, I thought, but held my tongue. At that moment, the door flew open and in swept Morag with the two boys. Roddy was three and a half by now and becoming quite independent, while Donald was a year old and beginning to walk on his own. My heart stopped when Donald toddled up to Colin and put his arms out. All men were daddy to him at that time. I quickly lifted him into my arms and took him away from Colin.

'Hello little Roddy. Look how you've grown,' Colin said, when he saw Roddy. 'Is this little one yours too?' he continued, nodding at Colin.

I felt my face grow pink. How would I convince him that Donald was ours given how sick Roderick had been when Colin was working for us?

'Yes. This is our Donald,' I said, smiling fondly and cuddling him close.

'Roderick must have made a quick recovery after I left to father such a handsome boy.'

What a cheek he had, casting aspersions on Roderick's manhood. He really was intolerable.

'He was on the mend before you left Colin, so it wasn't all that quick.'

I knew my words sounded defensive and took a deep breath to calm myself down. Surely, he wouldn't suspect anything. That would be the worst thing that could happen. I reassured myself that he couldn't possibly suspect anything. It was just my guilty conscience. Not that I had anything to feel guilty about. Colin had left Heather to fend for herself knowing she was pregnant, and Roderick and I had saved the situation. How I wished he would just leave.

'Is there anything I can get for you, Colin? Stamps, a postal order perhaps?'

'No, no. I just came in to inquire after Heather.'

There was a short, awkward silence while we stood, not knowing what else to say.

156

'Well, I'll take my leave of you now. I'm heading out to the front after Christmas. Wish me well.'

'Of course,' I said, crossing the fingers of one hand behind my back, while I shook his hand with my other one as I wished him anything but well.

When I told Roderick about Colin that night when we were having a pre-bed cup of tea and the children were settled in bed, he was livid.

'The cheek of that man, having the gall to ask after Heather.'

'I was a little flustered when he asked what had happened to Heather, and then when Donald came in and ran up to him, I nearly fainted. What do you think he would do if he suspected Donald was his?'

'Run a mile, as he would not want people to know. It would ruin his reputation such as it is.'

'I hope you're right, Roderick. We are settling in nicely here and I would hate for there to be trouble.'

We had settled in nicely. For the first couple of months after we arrived back in North Uist, we had lived with my mother and father. Living conditions were cramped and Roderick couldn't help much on the croft. I did what I could, but we felt we were imposing so it was a relief when the post office jobs became available even though it had been because of the war. I'll never forget the look of fear on my mother's face when a neighbour rode up to tell us they had put a notice up outside the post office.

Everyone knew that Prime Minister Asquith had given the Germans an ultimatum to get out of Belgium by midnight on 3rd August, but they did not, and war was therefore declared. Mother's face was as white as the sheets billowing in the wind. We had all discussed the implications of war, so she knew her sons could be called on to fight. Father would be classed as an essential worker, as he would help to feed the population, so she would still have him. Of course, Johnny and Lachlan were excited at the prospect of leaving the island and visiting other countries as well as donning

157

the uniform of the Queen's Own Cameron Highlanders. It didn't seem to occur to them that in exchange, they would need to fight.

Morag had come to live with us at the post office to help with the children and the housework while I was working. It suited her to live closer to the Lochmaddy Hotel, where she had an early start. Roderick's health had improved considerably since coming home, and he seemed to be much calmer and happier. We decided not to have a photograph of Heather on display, as it would only lead to awkward questions that we didn't want to answer. Everyone accepted both boys were ours and no one commented that Donald's skin was slightly darker than his brother's. They both had Roderick's bright blue eyes, which helped, but after seeing Colin that day, I had noticed Donald had the same dimpled smile as Colin. I didn't tell Roderick though as I didn't want to cause him any unnecessary stress now that his health was recovering. We hadn't discussed what we would tell Donald when he was older. Was it fair to let him know we weren't his actual parents, or would it be kinder to let him think we were? Did it matter? So long as he was healthy and happy, that was all that was important. I felt sure that Heather would have been content with whatever we decided.

CHAPTER FORTY-FOUR

It was 1916 before Colin entered my life again and at the time, I was glad he did. Life was busy running the post office. We had to sort the mail ready for collection or delivery when it landed from the mainland by the boat. We were the first to know what was going on in the war effort as we received a telegraph from London every Saturday, giving an update on what was happening in the war. It was our job to post it up outside the post office on Sunday mornings, so after church on Sunday had become a meeting place for the islanders wanting to share news on the war and talk about their loved ones who were fighting. The newspapers reported that there had already been many casualties because of the new-fangled weapons that the Germans and the Allies had developed. These included flying Zeppelins and gas to fight the conflict and they reported that it was a war unlike any other that the world had ever before experienced.

Delivering telegrams to families whose loved ones had been killed or were missing was our responsibility, too. There was some hope if they had been reported missing, as it could mean they were still alive and a prisoner of war, but from what Johnny told us when he was on leave, many men were blown up in No Man's Land and would never be found. He had described in detail the terrible devastation that they were living and fighting in. The fleas, the rats as large as cats, the stench of decomposing bodies lying in No Man's Land with no hope of a decent burial. Not that he had told me or Mother, but I had heard him speaking to Father and was glad that Mother hadn't heard him. She would have been even more distressed about her boys had she known.

I hated delivering the telegrams. I was a well-known figure in my post office issue uniform of tarpaulin coat, stout boots and a wide-brimmed hat so I knew that anyone who had a husband, son or daughter working for the war effort in foreign lands, would dread seeing me approach in case I was delivering bad news. In other parts of the country, the telegram boys, who the post office had

159

specifically employed to deliver these messages of doom, were known as the Angels of Death, so I suspected that I might have the honour of that title too.

We were two years into the war now and both my brothers were fighting somewhere in Europe. Letters were censored, so we never knew exactly where they were, but we always made sure we sent them little parcels and letters to help keep their spirits up. Janet had left the Factor's house to train as a nurse in Glasgow. She wrote little about what she saw in her infrequent letters, but reading between the lines, I knew it must be bad. Janet liked to gossip and would normally like nothing more than telling me stories about the boys who were being brought in, so I knew there couldn't be many cheerful stories that she could share. The papers were also full of the casualties that we were sustaining and North Uist had its fair share of those.

It was coming up to Christmas 1916 and my mother hoped that at least one of my brothers would be home on leave, although she had received no news that they would be. We had only seen them twice since they went away to fight. Johnny had put on a brave face whenever he had been home, but Lachlan was quiet and withdrawn. I thought of them constantly and dreaded that one day we would receive a telegram telling us that one of them was missing, injured, or dead. That day arrived, but it was a slightly different telegram.

It was Roderick who took the messages that came through on the telegraph, and his face was grave when he handed them to me. It was lunchtime, and I had just closed the post office after a busy morning.

'Chrissie, sit down my pet. A message has come in about Lachlan.'

I felt my body grow cold. This was it. The telegram I had been dreading. My baby brother was dead.

CHAPTER FORTY-FIVE

'Oh Roderick, how can I tell *Mathair* and *Athair* that Lachlan is dead. It will devastate them.'

'He's not dead, Chrissie,' he said, handing over the telegrams. 'It's worse than that.'

I was puzzled. How could anything be worse than death? Had he been so severely wounded that he could no longer walk and look after himself? I had heard stories about soldiers who had been too gravely injured to function anymore. I took the telegrams from Roderick. One was for the constable and one for my father. The one for the constable told him that Lachlan was absent without leave and that he should search his family home to see if he was there and the one to my father told him that if Lachlan returned home, he should be handed over to the constable. I was struck dumb and could only stare at Roderick. This was shameful news. How could I deliver a message like this to my mother and father? White feathers were being handed out to men who were conscientious objectors and after the government introduced conscription in 1916, many of them were punished with imprisonment or sent to the front despite their objections. I dreaded to think how people would react towards Lachlan if they knew he had run away. The fighting was hard for everyone and people saw it as cowardice to abandon your post and your comrades.

'Oh Roderick. This is the most awful news. I better deliver the telegram to the constable right away and then go over to the croft and let *Mathair* and *Athair* know.'

'Hold on a minute, Chrissie. Take a breath.'

'But if we don't give the telegram to the constable, won't we be breaking the law?'

'I'm not saying don't give it to him. I'm just saying take some time to think about it before you do. What if Lachlan is there already? What will you do? Will you hand your own brother over to the constable?'

I sat down at the kitchen table and put my head in my hands. Could I? Little Lachlan, my sensitive little brother, who had helped round the croft uncomplainingly and who had willingly, at the age of just eighteen, volunteered to fight for king and country. How had it come to this?

'He must be terrified, Chrissie. The conditions at the front must be intolerable for him to run away. You saw how he was the last time, so pale and thin.'

I remembered. He hardly spoke and spent all his time scribbling in a notebook that he carried with him everywhere. When I had asked to see it, he told me it was better if I didn't. There were things in his notebook he would not want me to see. How I wished I had insisted and spent more time trying to get him to talk. He was no longer the carefree youth who had swaggered off proudly in his uniform; he was a war-weary soldier who was finding it all too much to cope with. Perhaps if we had realised how bad it was for him, Father could have asked Doctor MacInnes to issue him with a sick line and he could have got some respite. I looked at Roderick and asked him what I should do.

'I don't know, my love. I just want you to think about it before rushing in. Is there anyone you could speak to about it who might give you advice? Your family would be guilty of harbouring a fugitive if you covered for him and might face prosecution. I think it would be best if you could find out what the law is before telling your parents.'

'Should I speak to the constable when I deliver the telegram? Perhaps he could tell me the rights and wrongs of what we can do.'

'I'm not so sure. He may make his way to the croft right away, and if Lachlan is there, your father would be in trouble. I was wondering whether Victoria might help you. Her brother is an officer in the army after all so they must talk about these things.'

Of course, Victoria. She and I had become close friends since Roderick and I had returned to North Uist, but the thought of Colin knowing about Lachlan was not one I relished. Could I perhaps just ask her hypothetically the questions I needed answers to without giving away that it was for our family?

'Will you cover the post office Roderick while I walk over to see Victoria? I need to find out what the situation is as soon as possible. We don't want to delay delivering the telegram to the constable too long. We would lose our jobs here and that would be a disaster.'

'Of course. You go now and I will cover.'

CHAPTER FORTY-SIX

It didn't take me long to walk over to see Victoria as the Factor's house wasn't far from the Post Office but my heart was pounding and I was breathless by the time I arrived. I banged on the door and was disappointed when Mrs McAllister opened it. She still treated me as if I were a servant of the house.

'What's your hurry Chrissie MacIntosh? Has someone died?

Her face changed when she saw the look on my face and realised what she had said. I took some satisfaction in seeing her blush deeply.

'No, don't worry Mrs McAllister. I'm not here on official business, but I need to see Miss Victoria as a matter of urgency.'

'She's with Master Colin just now. He's home on leave.'

My heart sank. He was the last person I wished to see. I wouldn't be able to talk to Victoria with him in the room. I wouldn't trust him with the news I had to share with her. Luckily, as I was trying to decide what to do, I heard a commotion behind Mrs McAllister and Colin calling her name.

'Mrs McAllister, I am going out for a ride and my sister requires afternoon tea. Can you see she gets it please?'

'Yes sir,' she said, turning back to me.

'Please Mrs McAllister. Please ask Miss Victoria if she will see me.'

Opening the door wider, she asked me to pass through.

'Wait here and I shall ask her.'

I was on tenterhooks, pacing up and down the hall while waiting, so didn't notice Colin coming back.

'What are you doing here?' he said, as he came up behind me. I noticed he had a small scar on his cheek and was limping.

'Colin. I didn't know you were home. How are things with you?'

'As well as you would expect in current circumstances, Mistress Macdonald, but you haven't answered my question.'

'I've come to pay a visit to your sister.'

'Don't you have work to do in the post office? I thought it was a very busy occupation, especially during the war.'

'Yes, it is, but I do get some time off. Roderick is covering for me.'

'And how is your husband? Much recovered?'

'Of course. I told you he became much better not long after you left.'

Before we could continue our conversation, Mrs McAllister called to me.

'Miss Victoria will see you now. I shall bring you some tea. You know where to go.'

'Thank you Mrs McAllister. Goodbye Colin,' I said.

'Goodbye Chrissie. It was lovely to see you again,' he said, holding out his hand, which I reluctantly took. He then had the gall to raise it towards his lips. When I pulled it away, he laughed and went on his way. He really was an insufferable human being. I couldn't believe that Miss Victoria was his sister. She was such an agreeable person.

'Good afternoon, Chrissie. It's always lovely to see you, but I wonder what has brought you here today. Mrs McAllister said you seemed rather perturbed,' Victoria said as she poured our tea.

'Hello Victoria. Yes, I am and I'm afraid seeing your brother hasn't helped.'

'Oh, you bumped into Colin. It's a pity that you and he could not repair the damage he caused before you left for Canada. I feel that fighting in France has changed him. He has been involved in the Battle of the Somme for these last few months and has been telling me of the terrible casualties our army is sustaining. What he tells me is so different to what the papers are reporting. I worry so much for his safety. Anyway, enough of my brother. Tell me what's troubling you.'

'It's Lachlan, my youngest brother. We have received a telegram for the constable telling him that Lachlan is absent without leave and that he should visit the croft to see if he is there.'

She stopped to stare at me, her cup halfway to her lips. 'Oh Chrissie, that's a really serious offence. But why have you come to talk to me about it?'

'I wondered if Colin had discussed with you anything about what happened to a soldier when he deserted and if there was anything that we could do to help Lachlan.'

'You know he can be court martialled and shot. There is truly little sympathy for deserters.'

'I know that from reading the newspapers, but what if he is ill? The last time he was home, he was withdrawn and hardly spoke. I could see that something troubled him, but he refused to talk about it. If he does come home and my parents gave him shelter, would they be guilty of a crime?'

'I think they would be. He is a deserter, after all. It is strange, but Colin was just talking about this very subject. He said lots of the men are suffering on the front. They seem unable to stand the noise from the constant shelling. But he says they get little sympathy. The doctors tell them that if they don't go back and fight, they will be shot.'

'But some of these boys are so young. Lachlan was only eighteen when he signed up. Surely they would show mercy.'

'Colin says they can't afford to. They need to set an example so that desertion and mental sickness don't become acceptable. They could lose too many soldiers if they did, as the conditions are so horrendous. Colin has received an injury himself, as you may have noticed, but he only received a brief period of sickness leave to recover. He has now been made up to captain and will be going back soon to lead a new group of men at the front. There are so many officers losing their lives or being injured, they move up the ranks quickly. I can tell he is dreading it but he puts on a brave face.'

Her lip quivered as she thought about her brother fighting back at the front. Oh, how I sympathized with her.

'What are you going to do?' she said, looking at me with tears shining in her eyes.

'I will need to deliver the telegram, of course, otherwise Roderick and I would be guilty of interfering with the mail, but I need to warn my parents. They will be so upset.'

'If there is anything I can do to help, please just ask.'

'I will Victoria. You are a dear friend. Thank you for listening to me.'

'Do keep in touch and let me know what happens with Lachlan,' she said, hugging me goodbye.

CHAPTER FORTY-SEVEN

I picked up my bike from the post office and cycled over to the croft as soon as I left Victoria, but only my mother was in. My father was out working.

'Hello Chrissie. What brings you here today? Aren't you working?' She was busy preparing vegetables for broth.

'I have some news *Mathair*.'

She stopped what she was doing and sat down at the table, still holding the knife she had been using in her hand.

'You've received a telegram. Which of my boys is it?' she asked, tears forming in her eyes.

'It's Lachlan, but he's not dead *Mathair*. It's worse than that. He is absent without leave.'

'Absent without leave? What does that mean?'

'He has deserted his post *Mathair*.'

The tears that had formed spilled over on to her worn cheeks and she just stared vacantly at me. She had no words. Her baby boy was doomed. She knew it and I knew it. We sat in this silence for I don't know how long, and then she rose and continued with her chopping and slicing.

'*Mathair*. I need to deliver the telegram to the constable and if Lachlan does by some miracle get here, you cannot shelter him.'

'Chrissie. You are a mother. Do you think I could turn away my son? You must do what you must do and leave me to do what I must do.'

'Of course, *Mathair*. Will you be alright on your own?'

'I am not on my own. God is with me,' she smiled. 'His will be done.'

I envied her unquestioning faith.

I then delivered the telegram to Constable Morrison. It was the second telegram I had delivered to him, but the first had been as a father, not as an officer of the law. At the beginning of the war, he had been a jolly rotund man, but losing his son to this war had turned him into a frail figure with no joy left in him. When he read the telegram, he looked up at me.

'Chrissie, if Lachlan comes here, I will need to call the military, you do understand that?'

'Yes, sir, I do. I have explained it all to my *mathair,* but I fear that if Lachlan arrives, she will not turn him over to you.'

'Well, if he turns up, don't tell me. What the eye does not see…,' he smiled and winked at me, looking for a moment almost like his old jolly self. 'But if I see him, then I will have no choice, much as it would break my heart to do such a thing.'

'I thought you might have been angrier, sir, because of what happened to Jamie. He was killed in battle fighting for his country and my brother has deserted his post and left others to do the fighting. Yet you seem to have some sympathy for him.'

He sighed.

'If I could have Jamie back alive, I wouldn't care if he had deserted his post. Nothing is black and white, Chrissie, nothing in this damned, hellish war is black and white. Who knows what horrors he has endured? A man can only take so much. But I am angry, Chrissie. Don't be fooled. I am so angry; I want to scream sometimes. Not at the boys fighting on the front, or the men who can take no more, or the men who object to the whole bloody thing, but at the futility of it all and at the officers who compel the men to go over the top day in and day out while they sit by planning their strategies. I'm angry that it would be me who would have to betray a friend and hand over a young lad I have known since he was a baby.'

Tears were trailing down his ruddy cheeks as he turned from me and closed the door. I felt a sense of relief that it had not outraged him about Lachlan running away. Patriotism was running high, and few people held the same views as Constable Morrison. My heart was sore at the thought of Lachlan all alone somewhere, fearing that he would be caught and sent back, or worse. If only he could get home to the island, perhaps we could hide him and keep him safe until the war ended. Surely after the fighting was over, they would not court martial him and execute him. That was only in times of war. I looked up at the sky where dark clouds were gathering and knew the rain would soak me on my way back home via the croft, but it was a small price to pay. I needed to let Mother know the constable was on our side.

CHAPTER FORTY-EIGHT

It took Lachlan another two weeks to reach us. Not that I knew anything about it. Mother and Father kept Roderick and me out of it for fear that we would lose our jobs, or worse. Normally, I visited the croft at least once a week, but Mother began to visit us on a Sunday after church, saying that it was too much for us to visit them on top of our jobs.

'You and Roderick are busy, Chrissie. What with working and looking after these little boys of yours,' she said, smiling fondly over at Roddy and Donald.

But there was a feverish air about her and I wondered if the situation with Lachlan was affecting her mind. Mother was always so steady, but nowadays she was edgy and impatient. When I said it was no problem to visit the croft, she shouted at me just to do as I was told. It wasn't until one of our neighbours, Mrs Campbell, came into the post office to post a parcel to her sister in Edinburgh, that I realised Lachlan must be home.

'Good day to you, Mrs Campbell. Lovely day, isn't it?'

'Yes, it is Chrissie. I want to post this parcel today. My sister lives in Edinburgh and fresh foods are in short supply, so I like to send her some eggs or a chicken now and then.'

'I know Mrs Campbell. My aunt lives in Glasgow and she loves when my mother sends her something from the croft.'

'Aren't we lucky to live on this island and have access to the beasts that we rear and the crops that we grow? It sometimes feels that we aren't at war.'

That was easy for her to say and I would have loved to disagree, but she was a customer. Her son hadn't needed to fight as she was a widow and she needed him to work on the croft. How I wished Lachlan had stayed and did that. Her next words made me wonder if she had read my mind.

'Your father must miss the help of your brothers. I see he had someone working with him the other day.'

'Oh, did he? Who was it? Young Callum?'

'No, not Callum. If I didn't know better, I would have said it was your Lachlan, but it can't be him, can it? He's away fighting.'

My face must have given my feelings away.

'Are you alright, Chrissie? You've gone as white as a sheet.'

'I'm alright Mrs Campbell. I just feel a little faint. Sorry. Can I help you with anything else now?'

'No, no. That's all for today. You have a break now. You look like you need a cup of strong sweet tea. You've not been feeling sick in the mornings, have you?' she smiled at me knowingly.

I smiled back. She obviously thought I was with child again and it was better she gossiped about that to our neighbours than the truth of the matter. No one must suspect that Lachlan was here. Although no one knew he had deserted - only the constable was aware of that and he had kept that news to himself - it would be disastrous if they thought he was home on leave. Whenever any of the boys came on leave, everyone made a fuss of them as befitted the heroes that they were, so it would be impossible for us to conceal his presence from the constable and he would need to act.

Luckily, it was almost closing time, so I shut up early. I needed to talk to Roderick. It was all clear now why Mother had been discouraging us from visiting the croft. My heart was beating fast and my hands shook as I locked away the money, stamps, and postal orders. I felt sick. What were we going to do? Mother and Father couldn't keep him hidden indefinitely, especially now that Mrs Campbell had spotted him. I thought of my mother's faith in God and prayed earnestly for Him to guide us and save my little brother.

172

CHAPTER FORTY-NINE

Roderick and I agreed I should cycle over to the croft to find out what was going on, as it was best that he shouldn't be involved at any level just in case we were found out. When I arrived, my mother came out. I was absolutely soaked with the driving rain and was looking forward to getting in out of the storm that had blown up. So, I was taken aback when she told me to turn around and go back home.

'I am not going home, *Mathair*. I know that you have Lachlan here. Mrs Campbell told me she saw someone who looked like Lachlan out in the fields. You need to let me come in. I'll catch my death if you don't.'

'What do you mean, Mrs Campbell saw him?' her voice yelled over the wind and rain. I could see that she was frightened. 'She can't have. He's been inside since he arrived. We haven't let him out.'

'Well, he got out somehow *Mathair* and Mrs Campbell spotted him.'

'It will be all over the island by now. That woman is a terrible gossip. What are we going to do?'

I set the bike against the wall and mother ushered me inside.

'Come in, come in Chrissie. I'm sorry. I wasn't thinking straight. Take your wet things off.'

I could hear a movement through the other side of the curtain where I used to sleep with Morag in the old days. It was only six years ago, but it seemed like a lifetime.

'You better come through, Lachlan. Chrissie is here to tell us that Mrs Campbell has spotted you.'

A young man I hardly recognised pushed the curtain to one side and came through. Lachlan had always been slightly built, but he was stick thin now and his clothes were hanging loosely on him. Where had that dashing young man who had gone to war only a couple of years ago disappeared to? His skin was pale, and he had dark circles under his eyes, one of which seemed to have a

173

perpetual twitch. While mother busied herself making tea, I opened my arms wide and my little brother collapsed into them. We stood and wept together, our bodies shuddering in harmony with the heartbreak of it all. Mother put her arms around the two of us and then drew us gently towards the table and the scalding hot tea that she had laid out with oatcakes and crowdie.

'Come, eat now. The tea will heat you up, Chrissie. Your *Athair* will be in soon. We will discuss what's to be done when he arrives. I'll away out to see to the chickens while you and your brother have a catch up.'

I munched on the oatcakes and crowdie and relished the heat from the tea, but Lachlan just moved the food around his plate, his eyes following his hand as if it were the only thing in the room.

'Lachlan, do you want to tell me what's been happening? I won't judge you, I promise.'

He looked up at me then, his pale blue eyes looking even paler than normal and red rimmed from crying. I noticed he had a rash on his hands that he kept rubbing.

'You are the only one who won't judge me, Chrissie. Everyone else will just think I'm a coward and that I don't want to fight. But it's not that I don't want to fight, it's that I can't.'

He put his head in his hands and shook it from side to side as if trying to loosen something in his brain.

'I can't stand the noise. There's something wrong with my ears but everyone says I've just to get on with it. As a warning, they even made me take part in a firing squad against one boy who had run away and was caught. He was only the same age as me. I'll never forget it. Having to shoot at one of our own.'

He stood up now, pushing his chair roughly back from the table, and began pacing the room.

'That's what I'll face Chrissie, a court martial and a firing squad. You do not know what it's like. The constant gassing and shelling and dead bodies. I couldn't take any more. That's why when they shipped us to London for some leave, I ran away and came home. I wanted to see *Athair* and *Mathair* before I died.'

174

Just as he said this, Mother and Father came in.

'No one is going to die if I can help it,' my father said, grabbing Lachlan to him and encircling him in his brawny arms. 'Do you hear that mac? You are home now and no one is going to take you away from us.'

Despite his encouraging words, I was afraid that no matter how strong his arms, my father could not stop the force of the military.

CHAPTER FIFTY

Unbelievably, it was Colin who helped us with Lachlan. I had just unlocked the post office door when in he strode, as usual, looking full of himself, but I noticed his limp was more pronounced than when I had last seen him.

'Good morning, Colin. You are early this morning. What can I help you with today?'

'It's more, what I can help you with, Chrissie.'

I looked at him, puzzled. What could he mean?

'Victoria told me about your brother, Lachlan.'

My heart sank. Why on earth had Victoria told Colin about Lachlan? He was part of the military establishment, an officer. He would not look too kindly on a deserter.

'Did she?'

'Yes, and I have come to offer some advice if you wish to hear it.'

'Anything that would help my brother I will gladly hear.'

'Have you heard anything from him yet?'

'No, not yet.' I lied.

Perhaps he was telling me he could give me advice so that I would confide in him about Lachlan and then he would arrest him.

'What kind of man is your brother?'

'What do you mean?'

'I mean, does he agree with the war? Did he go to fight willingly or was he one of those conscientious objectors?'

'He certainly wasn't a conscientious objector. He went willingly to fight for King and country. Why do you ask? What difference does it make?'

'I am just trying to make sure that he is worth saving, that he is not just a malingerer who can't be bothered with the hellish conditions at the front. They are hellish for us all but we must put aside our personal feelings and fight the good fight.'

'He's not a malingerer, Colin. Please share this advice that you have.'

'Well, if a doctor can certify him as suffering from battle fatigue or the effects of gas or some other wound that is affecting his mental capacity, it would go a long way to helping prevent him being court martialled. I could also write a letter of support for him to go with the certification of the doctor.'

'You would do that? Why?'

'I feel bad at the way I left you and Heather to cope while Roderick was still unwell and I would like to make it up to you.'

I still didn't trust him, but his suggestion about the doctor made sense and if he was prepared to write a letter before he knew Lachlan was at the croft, then I was prepared to accept it. It was only a matter of time before Mrs Campbell would let slip that she thought she saw Lachlan, and then the constable would need to become involved.

'Do you think Doctor McInnes would do such a certification?'

'Well, I could have a word with him, but of course, he could only do it by examining and talking to Lachlan face to face. Do you think he will come back here?'

'I don't know. We have heard nothing from him yet. If only he would get in touch, we could tell him what you've said. Could you do the letter now Colin so that I can send it to him to use if he makes contact? I could type it up on the Remington and you could sign it.'

My stomach was churning at being beholden to Colin Donaldson, but at last I felt a small glimmer of hope for Lachlan's future. I couldn't deny him a chance of being saved because of my prejudices. He looked at me curiously.

'You seem overly eager to get me to do this letter. Why is that?'

What could I say that would be logical and still make him think we hadn't heard from Lachlan?

'Well Colin, you will go back to the western front and we won't be able to get in touch with you.'

I could have added 'and you might be killed and we won't get the letter' but thought better of it.

'Yes. You're right, Chrissie. It would be better if I did it now. I might be killed and then you wouldn't get the letter and that wouldn't do, eh!'

I blushed. Was the man a mind-reader now?

'Don't talk like that, Colin. I'm sure you'll come back unharmed.'

But no one knew who would come back or who would die in France and Belgium.

'Look,' he continued. 'I think the letter would look better if I put it on the headed notepaper that my father keeps for official business. It would look more authentic and official, would it not, than on just any old plain paper?'

'Yes, you're right. I suppose there's no rush until we hear from him, but it would be good to have it before you go back.'

'Of course. I'll send a message when it's ready. Goodbye for now.'

CHAPTER FIFTY-ONE

When the children were in bed that night, Roderick and I discussed the offer that Colin had made. At the mere mention of Colin Donaldson, Roderick became angry and was dead against taking anything from him.

'I want nothing from that man. He's the reason Heather is dead. Have you forgotten?'

'Of course, I haven't forgotten, but I think Colin feels bad about Heather. He had tears in his eyes when I told him that Heather was dead.'

'Tears! You are too trusting, Chrissie. Don't you remember the false tears he shed when he told you that his sister was dying and he had to go home. That turned out to be one big lie, didn't it?'

I nodded. By this time, I was in tears. I hated when Roderick shouted at me. I felt he was blaming me for bringing Colin Donaldson into our lives and Heather dying, and maybe I was. I lay in bed some nights wishing that I could go back and change everything that had happened, but I couldn't. But what Roderick was saying was giving me things to consider. I had trusted Colin when we were in Canada because I thought I had no other choice and here I was in the same position, only it was my brother that needed help.

'Roderick, please don't get angry with me. I'm only telling you what he told me. We don't have to take his help if you think it's the wrong thing to do.'

His face and voice softened. I knew he hated to see me upset.

'Why would that man want to help your family?'

'Perhaps the war has changed him, Roderick. Look at the effect it has had on Lachlan. Perhaps Colin is genuinely sympathetic to his plight. Perhaps he's felt like running away himself.'

'Yes, and I bet there would be no court martial and firing squad for the likes of him if he did. It's only the boys with no status and no money like your brother that are punished.'

179

Roderick was off again, ranting against the unfairness of society and how it was still manifesting itself in this war.

'I wish to God we had stayed in Canada. Coming back here just brings back the inequalities in British society between the haves and the have nots. At least in Canada there was an element of equality.'

I decided not to remind him that there was little equality for the native Indians, who were treated differently from the European settlers.

'But we are here, Roderick, and I am glad that we are. My *Athair* and *Mathair* would have had to deal with Lachlan's situation all on their own. At least we are here to help them.'

'You're right *mo ghraidh*. Sorry for going on. It's not helping, but it makes me feel better getting all these angry feelings out.'

He smiled, stood up and pulled me into his arms, and kissed me gently.

'Let's talk rationally now. So, what do you want to do? I think the idea of speaking to the doctor is good. Perhaps your *Athair* could do that. He's known Doctor McInnes for a long time.'

'Yes, that suggestion was the one that gave me most hope, but I wonder if he would need to be examined by an army doctor rather than a civilian doctor.'

'I expect he will, but it would lend some weight to his case for leniency if one doctor supported him to begin with.'

'What about the letter from Colin? Should we accept it? We would be beholden to him and I don't like to think of that.'

'You're right Chrissie. I wouldn't want to be beholden to him either, but if it helps Lachlan and you can get the letter and give nothing in return, then I say take it.'

'Thank you, Roderick. You are very grumpy sometimes but you always come round in the end.'

CHAPTER FIFTY-TWO

When I told my mother and father what Colin had said, like Roderick, they were suspicious.

'Do you think he knows Lachlan is here and is setting a trap to catch him?'

'No, I don't think so, but I don't know why he is offering to help us. He hasn't asked for anything in return and has promised to give me the letter before he goes back to the front. He is having it typed up on his father's estate paper so that it looks more official. What do you think about approaching Dr McInnes?'

'I'm not sure. I don't know how he will react. He isn't strictly one of us,' *Athair* said, meaning he was an incomer to the island although he had lived here for years, 'and the more people who know that Lachlan is here, the more chance of him being caught.'

'Who is going to catch me?' asked Lachlan, coming out of the bedroom.

'Och no one. Hush now,' said Mother. 'Master Colin up at the big house has suggested that if you can get Dr McInnes to say that the war has affected you in the mind, then you might not receive a court martial. He has also offered to write a letter confirming you are of good character in his role as a captain. What do you think, son?'

'I think anything that will help me is worth a try. I cannot stay here indefinitely as it is only a matter of time until I am caught and you will get into trouble. Ask the doctor to visit, *Athair*, and I will put my case to him. I need to take this chance.'

So, my father asked the doctor to visit and after talking to Lachlan for the longest time, he agreed to write a report supporting Lachlan's state of mind on the condition that he would go with him and hand himself into the constable. The following is the report he wrote.

To Whom It May Concern

Having examined and spoken at length with Lachlan MacIntosh of Lochmaddy, North Uist, I believe he is suffering from battle fatigue and shell shock. Therefore, he was not of sound mind when he decided not to return to active duty. I have written this report hoping you will take it into account in any court-martial proceedings that you decide to pursue. It is my opinion that he has fought gallantly for King and Country and that now he would be of better use to His Majesty's government were he to be discharged to work on the family croft rather than sent back to active service. His father is finding it hard to produce what the government requires with none of his sons to help him. The young man has voluntarily handed himself to the local constable.

Signed by Dr Stuart McInnes this 20th day of December 1916.

He handed the report to Lachlan, who thanked him.

'Thank you, doctor. I appreciate very much what you have done. I will gather my belongings and come with you to the constable now.'

It was with a heavy heart that we all made our way to the police station. Roderick and the constable were waiting for us when we arrived. Word had obviously got out. To my surprise, Colin was also there with a stiff white envelope in his hand, which he passed over to Lachlan. He nodded at him and pressed his shoulder. It was an intimate moment of mutual respect and support that only men who had been through the hell of the trenches could share. I never found out what Colin had said in his letter, but in one way, it made a difference and in another, it did not.

Before he left, Lachlan handed me the notebooks I had seen him writing in.

'I won't need them where I am going, Chrissie. I know I shall never see you again,' he said, batting away my protestations with his hands, 'but I want you to know that you have been the best big

182

sister and you,' he said, turning to Morag who was standing quietly, 'the best little sister I could have had. Do what you wish with these notebooks. They have been my friends these last two years. I couldn't have got through without them.'

'I shall cherish them always, Lachlan. Thank you for trusting me with them.'

It was a grey drizzling morning the following day when the constable took him to Lochmaddy Pier to catch the ferry at 7 am. Despite the early hour, there was a small crowd standing around, waiting. Lachlan had his uniform on again and although it hung on him loosely, his appearance was that of a soldier going to war. He stood proud and held his head high. It was as if now that he had said goodbye to his family, he was happy to accept whatever fate awaited him. My heart swelled with pride at his bravery. Most people stood silently, but some called out good wishes and some called out 'coward' and threw white feathers at him. But he did not look at any of them. Mother and Father clung to each other, their tears merging with the drizzle as they watched their youngest child leaving them forever.

None of us believed the military would discharge Lachlan from the army and be able to come back home. He would either be shot as a deserter or he would be sent back to die in the mud, and so it was. He was not court martialled but was sent to a military hospital and after three months they posted him back to active duty. He never returned. We received a telegram telling us he had been killed in action, which I delivered to Mother and Father in the normal way. The only consolation they could take from his death was that he had died a hero and been mentioned in dispatches for his gallantry. I often wondered if he had acted so gallantly because he wanted to die and escape the hell of the trenches. I would never know.

CHAPTER FIFTY-THREE

It was nearing the end of the war before I saw Colin Donaldson again and it was then that I realised the price of him helping my brother. I received a message from Victoria telling me that the army had discharged Colin because of the seriousness of his injuries. He had spent three months in an army hospital but was now back home and he had asked to see me. She begged me to come as soon as I could, as he was in such a poor state of health. She feared he would not survive the week. When I told Roderick, he frowned.

'That man always brings trouble to our door, Chrissie, but I suppose if he is nearing death's door, then to visit him is the Christian thing to do. Perhaps he wants to confess how bad he was to Heather and to beg for forgiveness.'

'Would you forgive him if he asked you?'

'No, I'm afraid I wouldn't, but it is God who will judge him, not me, thankfully.'

'He did his best to help Lachlan, so I feel I owe him for that.'

'Yes, he did, my love. You go but be on your guard.'

I set off that evening. It was as light at 7pm as it was at the same hour in the morning. The midges were out in force though, but I was well covered up so wasn't bitten. It was a beautiful summer evening, and I enjoyed walking along the road with the lapping of the water against the shore to one side. I wondered why Colin wished to see me and could only assume it was something to do with Lachlan. I had no premonition of the devastation he was about to land upon us.

It shocked me when I saw him. He was lying in bed, the small pink scar on his cheek standing out against the paleness of his skin. His face was gaunt and his arms, which were lying outside the covers, were stick thin. A rash covered his arms that looked like the pink spots I had seen Lachlan scratching on his arms. His eyes were closed when the maid took me upstairs to his bedroom, but they fluttered open when I sat in a chair that she had placed at the side of his bed. There was a nurse in the room, but she left when I entered.

'Hello Chrissie,' he said hoarsely. 'Thank you for coming.'

'Hello Colin, I'm sorry to see you so poorly.'

'I want to see him.'

'See who? Roderick?'

'No, not him. My son, my boy.'

My heart skittered in my chest.

'What do you mean, Colin? You don't have a son. I think your injuries have affected your brain.'

'Please Chrissie,' he said, reaching his bony hand out towards me. 'I know little Donald is mine. I just want to see him and hold him before I die.'

'Donald is ours Colin. His birth certificate proves it. I don't know why you think he is yours.'

'When I was in France, I was fighting alongside a battalion of Canadian soldiers. One of them was Frankie McNamara. You remember he worked for you in Canada.'

When I said nothing, he continued.

'He told me all about what had happened to Heather. That she had a baby but died because of birth complications. I am so sorry. I never meant for any harm to come to her.'

'Why did you pretend Victoria was ill and run away then? You are a scoundrel of the worst kind, and it's your fault that our Heather is dead. I hope you die too.'

I sobbed this out before I had time to think about what I was saying, and my eyes darted in his direction to see the effect of my harsh words. To my surprise, he was gazing at me with tears coursing down his cheeks.

'I loved her, but I knew we could never have married. I also knew that Frankie was fond of her and if I wasn't there, then he might have a chance with her. It was best for both of us I left. I didn't know she was expecting a child.'

He was still lying. Of course, he had known that Heather was pregnant. That was why he had made up the story about Victoria. He gulped back a sob before continuing.

'I understand why you are angry with me. I am guilty as charged and will stand before my Maker soon to answer those charges, but before I go, I want to see my son. Surely that's not too much to ask?' He hesitated, then continued. 'I helped you when your brother was in trouble.'

So, there it was. The payment for him helping Lachlan. I was in his debt. But how could I bring Donald up to see him without arousing suspicion? What would I tell Roderick and how would I explain it to Victoria?

'I will need time to think about this, Colin.'

'That's something I have little of.'

He sank back onto his pillow and closed his eyes looking as if he were already dead.

CHAPTER FIFTY-FOUR

When I left Colin's room, the nurse was waiting for me and told me that Victoria wished to see me before I left. On the way to see Victoria, I asked the nurse about Colin's condition.

'Nurse, Colin seems very weak and confused. He seems to think he is dying and only has a brief time to live. Is he correct?

'It is difficult to say. He has suffered some very severe injuries and although he could in time recover sufficiently to live a near normal life, I fear he has given up and doesn't have the will to live.'

'That is so sad. He is only a young man still. Do you think my coming and talking to him would make a difference? He says he would like to see me and my boys again before he dies. He worked with us in Canada, you know, and grew quite fond of our little Roddy.'

'It can't do any harm, Miss. Here we are.'

As I went into the room, Victoria stood up awkwardly and walked unsteadily towards me. It shocked me to see her walking and I ran towards her in case she would fall.

'Victoria, you are walking. How?'

'I have these metal straps on my legs called calipers. I wish someone had recommended them to me years ago. I know I look clumsy and awkward, but they give me such a sense of freedom I don't care how I look. But tell me how you found my brother?'

'He seems very weak and confused. He says he wants to see me again to talk about Lachlan and his war experiences and wants me to bring my boys with me. He grew quite fond of little Roddy when he worked with us in Canada, so that may be why, or maybe he just wants some young life around him. He thinks he doesn't have long to live. What do you think Victoria?'

She burst into tears and almost fell into my arms as she moved forward to embrace me. When she was safely seated again, she spoke.

'I don't know what to think, Chrissie. He is exceptionally low because of his injuries and I believe he no longer wants to live.'

'What injuries could be so bad they would make a man want to die?'

Victoria hesitated and then told me.

'He has lost his manhood, Chrissie. He can never take a wife or father a child because of his injuries.'

Now I understood why he didn't want to live and why he wanted to see Donald. But what if he did live? If he couldn't have a child, he may want to take Donald away from us. He would want an heir to his father's estate. This was the worst possible news, and news that I had to tell Roderick as soon as possible. I took leave of Victoria quickly despite her desire to continue our conversation and walked home in double quick time. When I arrived, Roderick was pacing the room waiting for me, eager to hear why Colin wanted to see me.

'Well, what did he want?'

'Please sit down Roderick. I can see you're agitated and rightly so, but we need to be calm when we consider Colin's request.'

He let out a sigh and sat in the armchair in front of the fireplace, empty of cheering peats at this time of year, and looked up at me. But I could see that he was anything but calm by the way his fingers tapped rhythmically on the arm of the chair.

'Right, Chrissie, I am calm. What did he want?'

'He wants to see Donald. He knows he is Heather's son.'

'How can he know that? No one in Scotland knows about Heather.'

'When he was fighting in France, there was a battalion of Canadian soldiers and one of them was Frankie. They got talking, and that's how he found out.'

'Damn him. Does he mean to take Donald away from us?'

'I don't think so. He is at death's door, Roderick. He just wants to see him and hold him before he dies.'

Roderick stood up and began pacing again. I sat down and waited until I could no longer stand his toing and froing.

'I feel sorry for him. He's dying and granting a dying man's request is the right thing to do, don't you agree?'

Roderick at last stopped pacing and sat down opposite me.

'I would agree if it were anyone else. But that man. I hate him Chrissie. I'm ashamed to admit it but I do.'

'Are you saying no to his request then, Roderick? I will abide by whatever you say. You are Donald's grandfather, after all.'

He sat in silence for a long time, staring into the empty grate.

'If he really is dying, then I would grant his wish, but what will we tell people. Everyone will think it strange that he wants to see a child he doesn't even know. I don't want anyone suspecting that Donald isn't ours. It would be unfair to the wee one.'

'I agree Roderick and when Victoria asked me why Roderick had wanted to see me, I told her he wanted to talk about Lachlan and his experiences in the war and to see our Roddy again as he had grown fond of him when he worked for us.

He looked at me with a hopeless expression.

'Are you sure he is dying? By taking Donald to see him, we are admitting, are we not, that he has some claim on him?'

'I can only say he looks as if he is dying, but God may spare him. And if he does, you're right. We will have confirmed that we have lied about Donald's parenthood and he could use it against us.'

'It's late. Let's sleep on it and see how we feel in the morning.'

CHAPTER FIFTY-FIVE

When the next day dawned, we were still undecided what to do but after discussing it again as we were getting ready for the day ahead, we agreed I should visit Colin once and take both boys and say that it was Roddy that Colin wished to see.

'Do not admit to Colin that Donald is Heather's son. Make out that you are bringing the boys along as a favour to him, not because there is any truth in what he is saying. Did he tell you what had happened to Frankie?'

'No, he didn't. I shall ask him when I see him. I will go over on Saturday. Hopefully, he will live that long. I'll send Morag with a message today.'

I'm sorry to say that I forgot to ask him about Frankie in the emotion of him meeting Donald, something I was to regret later. I felt a little better now that we had made our minds up and am ashamed to say that part of me prayed he would die. I couldn't bear the thought of him trying to take Donald from us.

When we arrived on Saturday, I was sorry to see that Colin had slightly more colour in his cheeks than he had when I first saw him. As before, the nurse left us and asked me if I wanted her to look after the boys. It was a little awkward as normally that would have been the right thing to do, but the boys were only there for Colin's sake.

'No, that won't be necessary, nurse. Thank you. Little Roddy here is a friend of Colin's and it will be nice for them both to see each other again.'

I then told the boys to play with a toy I had brought along with me, while I spoke to Colin, which they did, happily unaware of the tension in the room.

'Thank you for coming, Chrissie, and for bringing him.'

'I have only brought him as a kindness because you have this delusion that he is your son and I wouldn't like to cause a dying man any more distress than is necessary. But let me be clear, Colin, this is the only time you will see Donald. It is important to protect his legitimacy, as you know how badly being illegitimate can affect a person's life. It would be a truly awful stigma for him to carry all his days.'

'Alright, Chrissie. Just give him to me now, please,' he said, looking longingly over at the boys.

'I will bring both the boys over now so that Roddy doesn't feel that Donald is being favoured over him and you must say nothing that would imply that Donald is your son, especially within earshot of Roddy. Do you understand?'

'Yes.'

'Roddy, bring your little brother over to see Master Colin. You remember Colin from when we lived in Canada, don't you?'

Roddy took his brother's hand, brought him over and peered at Colin.

'How do you do, sir? I'm afraid I don't remember you. I was only two when we were in Canada.'

Colin laughed lightly.

'Never mind, I remember you. Come and give me a hug if you don't mind and then I will give your brother a hug.'

Roddy climbed up onto the bed and submitted to the embrace that Colin gave him but looked relieved when he let him go and he went away happily to play with his toy. I then passed Donald over to Colin, who examined every inch of his face, no doubt looking for evidence that he was his. I checked Roddy wasn't looking at what was happening and saw that he was playing happily with his toy, totally oblivious to the drama unfolding. Colin then held Donald close, whispering 'my son, my son' into his ear until Donald began squirming to get down. I felt tears form in my eyes as I saw the love shining out of Colin's eyes for his son. If only he had stayed and accepted responsibility, everything could have been different. It was his own fault, only he was to blame for the current situation. However, I was finding it difficult to take Donald away from Colin, who was continuing to hold on to him despite Donald's protests, so I felt relieved when the nurse came in and said that Colin needed to rest now.

'Thank you, Chrissie,' Colin said. 'I shall die a contented man now. Take loving care of him, please.'

The nurse looked puzzled but said nothing, just ushered us out of the room. Fortunately, Victoria was busy, and we could take our leave without speaking to her. It would have been a difficult conversation.

CHAPTER FIFTY-SIX

Colin didn't die. We waited to hear of news of his death, but it never came. So, it was with a sense of foreboding that we read a letter from Victoria about a month after my visit.

Dear Chrissie,

I write to let you know the sad news that my father is ill and can no longer continue as Factor for the Laird. Colin will take over as Factor and has brought someone in to help him as he is not back to full health yet. I will move to our family home in Dumbreck in Glasgow to be with my father. Although we have been here for such a long time, it will be difficult to think of it as home again. I have become quite used to living in North Uist now and will miss its wild climate. I shall also miss you, Chrissie. You have been a good friend to me and to Colin over the years.

Colin is much improved since you last saw him. I am unsure what you talked about, but he seemed to turn a corner after you left. Something must have made him realise he still had a reason to live. In fact, he seems to be excited about something and has begun corresponding with our family solicitor. Letters have been flowing back and forwards between them, but Colin will not let me see the letters. He tells me I shall find out when the time is right.

With father unwell, it has made us both think about the future. It is a pity that neither of us will marry and have children which means my cousin Campbell Donaldson will inherit when Colin passes but father has ensured, by setting up a trust, that I may live in our family home for as long as I wish and will ensure I have sufficient income to live on. This gives me a sense of security. There are too many stories about women being abandoned to their fate by unscrupulous heirs.

We have made plans to remove from North Uist on the 15th of this month. It would be lovely to see you before we go, but I understand how busy you must be. Hopefully, this war will be over soon and we can all get back to normal living.

Your affectionate friend
Victoria

I was sorry to hear that Victoria was leaving as she was a dear friend and I would miss her. How I wished her brother would go back to Glasgow with her. He hadn't asked to see Donald again. I was relieved, but I wondered what he was corresponding with his solicitor about. Roderick was, of course, suspicious.

'The only reason he is in touch with his solicitor is because he is trying to find out how he can take Donald away from us. It is a strange coincidence that Victoria mentioned who will inherit when her father and Colin pass away.'

'But wouldn't he discredit himself if he claimed Donald as his child?'

'He doesn't care about his reputation. His behaviour has always been reprehensible. His ability to father a child and have an heir is more important to him now that he can no longer function as a man.'

I sensed an air of superiority in Roderick's words concerning Colin's manhood. The consumption had left no long terms effects in that regard for him, although we still hadn't produced another child, so perhaps it had affected his fertility somewhat if not his ability to enjoy intercourse. But I feared Roderick was right. Why else would Colin now have a strong will to live and be in correspondence with his solicitor when only a month ago he was on the verge of death?

'I think we should try to find out what our rights are Roderick.'

'But that will mean us admitting the truth about Donald's parentage. Although solicitors need to keep client business confidential, Mr Abernethy is indiscreet when he drinks and it's not the first time he has let slip something he shouldn't.'

'Why don't we ask Aunt Katie to contact a solicitor in Glasgow. She could say that she is asking advice on behalf of a friend who does not wish to disclose their identity at this stage.'

'But Katie doesn't know the truth, does she?'

'No, but I could go down to Glasgow and explain everything to her. It would be too difficult to go through it all in a letter and besides, the letter could be evidence against us if it fell into the wrong hands.'

'Can we trust Katie? Won't she want to tell your mother and father?'

'You know her better than I do, Roderick. What do you think?'

He looked at me, probably trying to guess whether this reference to their earlier relationship was a sarcastic barb or a genuine comment. I wasn't quite sure which it was. Part of me sometimes blamed Roderick for the situation we were in. If he hadn't agreed to come back and marry me, if he hadn't tried to save Lily, if he hadn't had the relationship with Lily, Heather would never have been born and Colin would never have had the chance to abandon her. But, if he and Katie had married, then none of this would have happened, so really it was Katie who was to blame. I sighed. It was fruitless going back over the past like that, trying to apportion blame. The situation was as it was and there was nothing we could do to change it.

'I thought she was a trustworthy person, Chrissie, but when she ran away to Glasgow and left me, I had to reverse that opinion. I know she had her reasons, but it was a selfish act that hurt her family. Who is to say that it wouldn't happen again?'

'Do we have a choice, Roderick? If Colin can take legal action against us, it will all come out anyway, so perhaps we need to tell our families just in case.'

'Let's put it off for a little while longer and see what happens. He hasn't asked to see Donald again so maybe we are worrying about nothing.'

CHAPTER FIFTY-SEVEN

We put Colin to the back of our minds and carried on as if we had nothing to worry about. We were making progress in the war. The Americans had joined the war effort last year, and it looked likely that things would work out in our favour. My brother Johnny came home on leave and was treated like a hero. We were all relieved to see that he bore no sign of the trauma that Lachlan had shown, although he spoke less about his experiences now than he had in the beginning. When I tried to tell him about Lachlan and the words he had written in his journal, he didn't want to talk about it.

'I don't want to talk about that while I'm here, Chrissie. I just want to relax and enjoy myself. Know any pretty girls who are looking for a handsome soldier?'

'Oh, so you think you're handsome, do you? Well in fact my friend Janet is coming to visit me, so why don't you come and have a meal with us. You never know, she might be desperate.'

He laughed and agreed to come along to dinner the following evening. I hadn't seen Janet since war broke out, so I was looking forward to a good catch-up. I didn't expect anything to happen between her and Johnny. They had known each other forever and had shown no attraction towards each other, but now that they had their war experience in common, who knew what might happen. But even if there was no attraction, there would be no shortage of conversation with my brother Johnny there. I hadn't read Lachlan's notes in full as the little I had seen made difficult reading, and I wondered how Johnny and Janet could overcome the horror of it and act normally. I'm not sure I would have been so strong.

We cobbled together an excellent dinner despite the rationing the government had introduced at the beginning of that year. My father contributed a hen, potatoes and butter while I got some flour and sugar to bake a cake. Johnny brought a bottle of whisky he had acquired somewhere on his way home and Janet brought some chocolate she had received from an American soldier she had nursed. I wondered if Roderick would allow Johnny and Janet to drink the whisky, as he was still strictly teetotal, but to my surprise, he got the glasses out and even gave Morag and me one. He stuck to water but was obviously enjoying the banter and laughter fueled by the alcohol. If there was a slight air of hysteria to our gathering, no one commented. The children loved having the company and were reluctant to go to bed and leave the party, as they called it, but they were both so exhausted that once in bed they fell asleep soundly. I couldn't help standing for a while looking at their sweet little faces. My heart would break if Colin took Donald from us. He was as much my child as Roddy was now.

Johnny walked Janet home, and I was unsurprised when Janet told me the following day that they planned to meet up in Glasgow the next time they had leave. Roderick and I waved them off, saying a silent prayer that God would keep them safe. That night I felt like a young girl again and made love with abandon the way I had done in the early days of our marriage all those years ago. Perhaps it was the whisky, but I think Roderick and I fell in love with each other again that night, but in a deeper, more mature way. There were no secrets, nothing to hide from each other. The next day, we decided we would seek legal advice. We were going to do whatever was needed to fight for our family.

CHAPTER FIFTY-EIGHT

I wrote to Aunt Katie asking if I could come and stay with her for a few days and asked if she could try to find a lawyer that I could speak to about a family matter. I told her I would explain everything when we met and would appreciate if she did not mention it to my mother when she was writing to her as I hadn't told her yet that I was coming to visit. She agreed, and I set off for Glasgow. I hadn't seen Katie since that time when Roderick and I stayed the night before travelling to Canada. At that time, I didn't know their history, but I did now and I wondered how I should broach the subject with her and what her reaction would be. What had it been like for her to decide to abandon her future husband and run away to Glasgow? She was only twenty back in 1896 and the position of single women in Scottish society was quite different to what it was now. The war had given women positions they could never have dreamed of holding back then. Poor Roderick, it must have been such a shock when he found out that he was going to Canada on his own and not as a married man. Hearing his account of how my father had betrothed me to him in exchange for the dowry he had paid for Katie still felt uncomfortable.

When I arrived in Central Station, I was not as overwhelmed as I had been that first time, although there was a feverish air of comings and goings with most passengers wearing soldiers' uniforms. There were many parting couples crying and clinging to each other, and I felt for them. After taking the time to read Lachlan's notes, I had decided that I would find a way to have them published. Hadn't Wilfred Owen had his poems published when he was recovering in Craiglockhart Hospital in Edinburgh, so I didn't see why Lachlan's poems couldn't be published too. He had experienced the horrors of war and had suffered because of them. If I could share his experiences, then perhaps other people would understand what they themselves were going through. They would understand that they were not cowards. I scanned the platform and at last saw Katie waving to me.

'Chrissie, my darling. How lovely to see you? Shall we get lunch before we go back to my house? You must be hungry after your long journey.'

'That would be lovely, thank you Katie.'

I didn't know what to expect. I had never been for lunch in the city and felt quite excited at the prospect.

'Let's go in here to the Central Hotel. They have a restaurant. Then we can return to Kinning Park on the subway close to where I live.'

I wondered what the subway was but guessed that I would find out soon enough. I had never seen anything so grand as the Central Hotel. It had revolving doors and a huge reception area with glazed arches which let the light shine in. A woman wearing a black-and-white uniform approached us and asked if she could help us.

'We would like a table for two please,' said Katie, as if this was something she did every day and perhaps it was for all I knew.

'Follow me, please.'

When we were seated in the small dining room, which was used for lunches, I felt slightly uncomfortable as I spotted the various pieces of cutlery on the table. I was used to a knife, fork, and spoon, but there seemed to be a variety of these utensils on the table and I wondered why there were so many. A stiff white cloth covered the table and there were large linen napkins folded into an elaborate shape sitting on a white plate inside the cutlery layout.

'This is lovely,' I said. 'Do you come here a lot?'

'It's my first time. It's posh, isn't it?'

I nodded, and we studied the menu, trying to decide what to order. We stuck to soup and sandwiches, but even that was expensive.

'Don't worry about the cost Chrissie, my treat,' she said, signalling to the server.

'Let's order and then you can tell me why you've come and what the family matter is that you want to discuss with the solicitor.

199

I've arranged to take you to see a friend of mine tomorrow who is training to be a solicitor.'

'A friend or a boyfriend?' I said, smiling at her as I knew women couldn't practice as solicitors.

'A friend. Her name is Maude Martin. She's been apprenticed to one of Glasgow's largest law practices and they have guaranteed her a job once she qualifies. A change in the law is underway, so she is confident that she will be able to practice.'

'She can't have much experience if she's an apprentice. Are you certain she can help me?'

'She is a very smart woman and when I said it was concerning a family matter, she told me that family law was one of the principal subjects she studied at Glasgow University.'

I was doubtful, but beggars can't be choosers. I wondered how Aunt Katie knew her, but the waitress appeared to take our order and I lost the moment to ask as I wanted to bring up Roderick before she came back with our food.

'Thank you, Katie. I appreciate you doing that. Before we move on, I would like to clear the air with you first.'

She looked puzzled, but I thought I saw the colour rise in her cheeks.

'I know about you and Roderick. I know you were meant to marry him, that my father had paid your dowry to Roderick, who had used it to pay for your fares to Canada, and I know you ran away to Glasgow before your marriage.'

'How did you find out? I don't imagine your father would have told you. He was so ashamed of me for letting Roderick down like that. He almost cut me off completely after that, but your mother talked him round. She said it was better to break off the relationship before the marriage as it would have been worse if we had married and had children.'

'But couldn't you have done it in a kinder way? To run away without telling him was cruel.'

'I know Chrissie, but remember I was young and if truth be told, I didn't have the courage to tell him to his face. They had arranged

200

everything. My brother, your father, had given him my dowry, and he had used it to pay for our passage to Canada. It just seemed such an enormous thing to do, so I took the easy way out and ran away. One of my friends had found a job in Glasgow and I turned up on her doorstep unannounced one day. She was a good friend. She took me in and helped me find work. I don't know what I would have done without her. It was a very selfish and stupid thing to do. I wish I could go back and change things, but I can't.'

'Do you wish you had married him?'

'No, I wouldn't have changed that, but I would have found a kinder of way of telling him he was not the man I wanted to marry. But look on the bright side. If I hadn't done what I did, then you and he would never have got together and had those two beautiful boys of yours.'

She smiled widely, but I could see her twisting the elaborate napkin while she was speaking. She needn't have worried. I would not berate her for her mistakes. None of us is perfect and anyone can make mistakes. I had just wanted to clear the air with her and that was it.

'That is true, Aunt Katie. So, thank you.' I said, thinking about our recent night of love.

The waitress arrived with our soup and we supped the posh consommé to the sound of the clinking of glasses and the scraping of cutlery. I thought the soup was rather over-priced and preferred my mother's broth, which was thick with vegetables and barley, to this watery liquid. When we had finished and the waitress had brought our sandwiches and a pot of tea, Katie looked at me expectantly.

'Well?'

'Where to begin?'

'At the beginning.'

So, I told her everything, in between munching the tiny triangled sandwiches with strange fillings and supping my tea, which was rather nice. Her face was a mirror of changing expressions with each stage of my story and when I reached the point of Heather dying, we were both in tears and had to use the napkins to wipe our cheeks.

'So, you think this Colin might want to take Donald away from you and will use the court to get him certified as his father?'

'I think so, yes. That's why I want to take some advice from the solicitor. I won't say it's me, but I expect she will guess it is. That's why I didn't want to use Mr Abernethy. Even if he didn't break our confidence, his secretary might.'

'What a difficult position to be in, but you don't need to worry about Maude. She is totally trustworthy. How is Roderick taking it?'

'He is livid. He hates Colin and the last thing he would want is for him to gain custody of Donald. He says we will fight him in the courts if we must, but I don't know how much that would cost and even if we could win if Colin gained evidence.'

'But where would he get the evidence? Everyone is in Canada.'

'I don't know Katie. That's why I need to speak to a solicitor to find out what he - sorry she - would do if she were acting for Colin.'

CHAPTER FIFTY-NINE

The next day, Aunt Katie took me to the house where her friend Maude Martin lived. It was in the west end of Glasgow and was much more substantial than the two rooms that Katie lived in. This woman obviously belonged to a wealthy family if she could afford to live in this area and I suppose if she could train as a solicitor, even if the law did not yet allow her to practice. However, when we went inside, it was clear the house was more than a place for living in. It was busy with women and thick with the smoke from their cigarettes. It was difficult to discern if the house was well furnished, as it was littered with books and papers.

Katie and Maude had become friends originally during the rent strike of 1915 in Glasgow and following that from their involvement in the women's suffrage movement. Evidence of that involvement was everywhere. There were posters urging the government to give women the vote, a typewriter with newsletters piled up next to it, and newspaper cuttings everywhere, showing the actions that the suffragettes had been taking to fight their cause. I could tell from the way Katie and Maude greeted each other that they were close friends. Maude was a lovely young woman slightly younger than me, but much more confident. She at once took control of the situation, and I was glad that Katie had told her a bit of the background.

'Come through to the back room, Chrissie. We'll be able to get some peace there. So, I understand you wish for some advice about a possible suit for paternity rights for your child, Donald Macdonald. Is that correct?'

'Yes, that's right Maude. Thank you for seeing me at such short notice. I do appreciate it.'

'Your aunt and I are close friends, and she has helped me on many occasions, so it is agreeable to be able to return the favour,' she said, taking Katie's hand and smiling at her.

Katie blushed, and I wondered fleetingly what a passionate friendship they must have. But I was here for Donald, and my thoughts moved on quickly to what I had come here for.

'My husband had a daughter, Heather, before he and I were married and I went to live with him in Canada. He became ill with tuberculosis and a man I knew from Scotland came to work for us while he was ill. He and Roderick's daughter entered a relationship that was kept secret from us. This man left to go back to Scotland at short notice and it turned out that Heather was pregnant. As there was no chance that she and the man would marry because of class differences, she agreed that Roderick and I should register the baby as ours so that no stigma would fall to her or her child. Sadly, Heather died when she was giving birth to Donald. We got our doctor to issue a birth certificate in our name.'

'How did you get the doctor to do this? Surely, he would have been breaking the law. Did your husband offer a bribe?'

'No. The doctor agreed because we were going back to Scotland to live permanently and it was unlikely that anyone would discover what he had done. He issued a birth certificate with the actual parents' names on it and gave us a blank form that we could fill in ourselves. In that way, no one could accuse him of doing anything illegal. He could just say that we stole the form from him.'

'What is the problem now?'

'The man was injured in the war and can no longer father a child. He met someone in the war who used to work with us on the homestead and he told him about the baby. So far, he has only asked to see the child on one occasion, but we have heard that he is corresponding with a solicitor and are worried that he is trying to find out if he can claim the child as his. If he did, then the little boy would become the heir to the family estate instead of a distant cousin. Are you able to tell me whether he can do that and what success he may have?'

'If it had been before 1915, I would have said it would have been almost impossible for him to prove that you and your husband were not the parents. Until then, the courts almost always accepted that if someone was claiming to be a mother, then they had given birth to the child and if the mother was married to the father, then it was assumed legally that he was the father and the child was legitimate.

'What changed in 1915?'

'In 1915, in the case of Slingsby v Slingsby the High Court of Appeal held that Teddy Slingsby was not the child of Mrs Slingsby but the son of another woman who had sold her infant to her and Mrs Slingsby had duped her husband into thinking that the child was his.'

'My goodness, how terrible.'

'In that case, it was Mr Slingsby's brother who contested the legitimacy of the child as it meant that the child would inherit the family estate, and he wished his brother's share of the estate to come to him rather than his brother's counterfeit son. Did you and your husband have anything to gain from claiming this child as your own?'

'No, as I said, we wanted to protect Heather's reputation and did not want the stigma of the term illegitimate to be put on Donald's birth certificate.'

'You know, the Registrar General has announced a change in the law regarding this and rightly so, as it is such a stigma. Children are no longer to be registered as illegitimate.'

'No, I didn't know that, but I am so glad. What a difference it will make to the children of unmarried mothers.'

'May I ask, if this man is wealthy and part of the upper classes, wouldn't it be in the boy's interests to live with his real father? Wouldn't he have a much better chance in life?'

'He is not a good person. Heather was only fifteen when he took advantage of her and we blame him for her death. We do not want Donald to be brought up by such a man.'

'Well then, that is a different matter. If he went ahead with a case against you and was able to prove that Donald was his son, you could lodge a counter case that he is an unfit father but whether the fact that he took advantage of Heather would be sufficient evidence or not remains to be seen. It is possible the courts may make your son a ward of court if they accept that this man is Donald's real father but is not fit to receive custody and then you would need to convince them you should have guardianship.'

My head was spinning with the different scenarios that Maude had set out, and I couldn't wait to go home and discuss it all with Roderick.

'There is so much to think about and it is possible that this man has no intention of trying to claim Donald as his own. Only time will tell. Thank you so much for seeing me. I cannot tell you how much I admire you, going to university and studying to be a lawyer. You are very brave. I wish you well and hope that the Government will change the law and allow you to practice.'

'Thank you. Goodbye and good luck. If I can be of any further help in the future, please let me know.'

CHAPTER SIXTY

I spent a very pleasant few days in Glasgow and found it an exciting place to be. It was so different from our island. The subway, which was a circular underground train that travelled round the city, was amazing although the smells and the wind that blew as we made our way in and out of the station was quite unpleasant. Katie took me to see a music hall performance and it was such fun. We even took a motorized taxi back from the theatre. After I told Roderick about all the exciting things I had done, we discussed what Maude had told me.

While we could possibly win a case that Colin was not a fit parent, the problem was that the truth would become public knowledge if there were a court case. When people found out that Roderick had fathered a child with a Cree Squaw, it would cause a scandal. Although it was commonplace in Canada for immigrants to marry native women, people in the Hebrides had little idea of what life was like in the prairies and would consider it a huge sin. We could not hold our heads up in public. It would also mean that we would need to tell our families and explain to Donald about Colin and Heather.

It was a predicament, and we talked round and round in circles, trying to agree what we should do. In the end, we waited to see if Colin would do anything, but we did not need to wait long. Within two weeks we received a thick manilla envelope from Mr Abernethy. It arrived the same day we received notification that the war had ended. While everyone on the island was overjoyed to read the news on our bulletin board, the contents of the letter consumed us so much we could not feel anything of the joy that others did. This is what the letter said.

Dear Mr Macdonald

I write to you on behalf of Mr Colin Donaldson. Mr Donaldson avers that you and your wife are not the natural parents of the child known as Donald Ewen Macdonald. He further avers that Mr Donaldson himself is the father of the said child and that the *mother was a girl called Heather Macdonald who died in Canada giving birth to the said Donald Ewen Macdonald on the night of 1st December 1913. He can furnish evidence to support his assertions and has a witness who will support his case.*

Mr Donaldson wishes to arrange a meeting to discuss the arrangements for handing over his son to his care, and I should be grateful if you would contact me to agree a suitable date. Furthermore, should you fail to attend such a meeting, Mr Donaldson has instructed me to raise an action in Lochmaddy Sheriff Court.

Yours faithfully

Abernethy & Company

Solicitors and Notaries Public

I gasped when I read the contents and looked at Roderick, whose face was motionless apart from a tick that pulsated on his cheek. He was obviously so infuriated at the contents of the letter that he could not speak.

'We are done for Roderick. He has appointed Mr Abernethy and is threatening us with court action here in North Uist. There is no way we will be able to hide what has happened. What are we going to do now? I can't bear to lose Donald. I just can't.'

'We are not going to lose Donald, not if I have anything to do with it. I'll kill him with my bare hands before I'll let him have our boy Chrissie.'

'Don't talk like that Roderick. I couldn't bear to lose you too.'

'I need some fresh air. I can't breathe.'

As he slammed out of the door, I collapsed onto the fireside chair and held my head in my hands and prayed to God to help us.

208

CHAPTER SIXTY-ONE

I was glad when Morag brought the boys back home from a walk as it stopped me wallowing in my misery, waiting for Roderick to return. There was an easterly wind blowing outside and their little faces were bright red with the cold. They were their usual boisterous selves, and I was glad of the diversion from my thoughts. Our family life was about to change one way or another, and I wanted to cherish every second I had left. I heated some broth, and we were all sitting at the table eating when Roderick returned.

'Just in time for lunch, I see. Good, it's freezing outside.'

I ladled some soup out for him and he sat at the table, chatting to Morag and the children. He seemed much happier, and I wondered what he had decided. After lunch Roderick opened the post office shop while I prepared sausages and vegetables for dinner. Several customers were waiting and there was an air of excitement about the news of the Armistice. My mother was there too. It was unusual for her to visit during the week, but she was excited about the news.

'Your brother will be coming home, Chrissie. I can't wait to see him.'

Neither of us mentioned Lachlan, but I was confident he was as much in my mother's thoughts as he was in mine. What a joy it would have been to be welcoming both my brothers home, but poor Lachlan was lying in a grave far from his homeland.

'Yes, it will be good to have Johnny home safe and well. There have been quite a few casualties from North Uist in this war, *Mathair*. It will be a relief not to worry about delivering telegrams anymore.'

'What about you and Roderick? Will the post office still employ you now that war is over?'

'The armistice has only just been signed, *Mathair*. We've hardly had a chance to discuss it yet, have we?'

I regretted the harsh tone in which I spoke. If only she knew that losing our jobs at the post office was the least of our problems.

'Are you alright Chrissie? You seem tense.'

'I'm fine. Sorry for being cross. I'm tired.'

I gave her a hug, and she kissed the boys and then set off home. She had got a lift in our neighbour's buggy. Like many others, he was coming into Lochmaddy so that he could read for himself that the war was over. He was now ready to go back home having had a gossip with the other people standing around outside the post office discussing the notice that we had put up.

At last, it was closing time and Roderick came through. He gave me a hug.

'Sorry about earlier. Once the children are in bed, we can talk.'

When the boys were safely tucked up, their little faces angelic looking in sleep, I sat down opposite Roderick.

'Have you reached a decision about what we should do, Roderick? You look so much happier than when you went out.'

'Yes. I've decided that I don't care what people say. We did what we did for a good reason. I think we need to find out what this evidence is that he has and who the witness is. I can't think who it could be, can you?'

'No. So far as I know everyone who knew us is still in Canada.'

'Let's agree to the meeting so that we can find out what he has, or whether he's bluffing.'

'Alright, I think that's an excellent suggestion, much better than wanting to kill him.'

'Yes, sorry. I do get a bit carried away when I'm angry, don't I?'

He smiled and my heart swelled. My Roderick was back to normal again.

'It's a pity we don't have the telephone here the way we had in Canada. We could have telephoned Katie and asked her to speak to Maude to find out what she thinks. I know she couldn't represent us but perhaps one of her male colleagues could.'

'Maude gave me her address and said I could contact her if I needed any further help.'

'Right, well why don't we send a telegram to Maude tonight telling her that the solicitor wants a meeting with us?'

'That's a good idea but we will need to tell our families, Roderick. We can't have other people finding out what Colin is trying to do before them.'

'I know. Let's visit them on Saturday and let them know.'

CHAPTER SIXTY-TWO

Morag agreed to sit with the children for a couple of hours while we went to visit my parents and Roderick's parents. The last thing we wished was for the boys to hear any of our discussions. Morag knew something was going on, but she didn't question us and I was grateful for that. When I came back from Canada, I still thought of her as an uncooperative, lazy girl and never thought she could be so industrious and helpful, but she had been a godsend these last few years. I knew she wouldn't stay with us forever as she had an ambition to go to Glasgow and train as a nurse, but luckily, she had agreed to stay with us until we could get someone to replace her.

I'll never forget how my mother and father reacted when we told them about Donald's parentage.

'Donald is not your son? I can't believe it. He looks like you Roderick. He has your eyes,' said mother.

'He is possibly my grandson. His mother was possibly my daughter.'

'Possibly, possibly. What do you mean? How can someone *possibly* be your daughter? Surely you must know.' My father's voice was controlled but ice cold.

'Your daughter,' my mother's voice screeched. 'But you never told us you were married. We would never have agreed to Chrissie marrying you if we had known.'

'I wasn't married.'

'Not married. Then how?' asked mother, who was now in tears.

Roderick looked at me, and as we had agreed, I told them all about Lily and Heather. With every word their faces registered how shocking this story was – guns, murder, squaws, illegitimate children – it was so out with their life experiences, they could hardly understand what I was saying.

'My poor girl. What a life you've had to live,' said father, suddenly looking old and shrunken.

'I am fine, *Athair*. Roderick is a good man and a good husband and father. I have suffered but haven't we all. You have lost your son in a bloody war. We lost Heather to childbirth. God gives, and He takes away. It is life.'

'Why are you telling us this now? Why did you not tell us in your letters from Canada? Why not when you came home? I don't understand.'

'You remember Colin Donaldson, *Mathair*?'

'I most certainly do. He tried to molest you at the Market in Lochmaddy. What has he got to do with it?'

'He came to work for us when Roderick was ill. I thought I mentioned that to you in my letters. But it doesn't matter now. The point is, he took advantage of Heather, then left her when he found out she was pregnant.'

'You mean Colin Donaldson is Donald's father? Good God! And he wants custody of Donald?'

'Yes.'

'Why does he want the child now?' my father said, patting my mother, who was now sobbing. 'Surely a man like that would not want to admit to taking advantage of a young girl and a young native girl to boot.'

Roderick then took up the story.

'He was severely injured in combat and is now unable to father a child. The only heir to the family estate would be a distant cousin, as Victoria is unlikely to have any children either. When he found out that Heather had died in childbirth, he figured out that the child must be his.'

'How did he find out? Who told him?'

'While fighting in France, he fought alongside a Canadian Battalion and it turned out one of the men was Frankie McNamara, who used to work for us in Canada. It was him who told Colin what had happened to Heather,' I said.

'Mr Abernethy is acting on Colin's behalf and has written inviting us to a meeting to discuss how we can hand Donald over to him. If we do not attend, Colin will raise an action in Lochmaddy Sheriff Court against us for custody,' continued Roderick.

'Mr Abernethy is representing him? It will be round the island in no time. The shame of it all, Angus. I don't know how I will face any of our neighbours.'

'Hush now Marion. You've done nothing to be ashamed of. We've got to think about little Donald and what is best for him,' said father.

Then, turning to Roderick, he asked 'What will you do?'

'We will go to the meeting as we think we will be able to find out more about what evidence he has. We have also asked a friend of Katie, who is training to be solicitor, for advice.'

'Good luck to you both. You will need it.'

CHAPTER SIXTY-THREE

We contacted Mr Abernethy to say that we would welcome a meeting, but that we were taking some legal advice of our own first and would contact him when we were ready to meet. This gave us time to hear from Maude, who sent a telegram saying that she would be happy to attend the meeting with us. The meeting took place in Mr Abernethy's office the week before Christmas 1918. Whatever would happen, it was unlikely to be a happy Christmas for us. We had discussed the situation with Maude and in the end, we felt we should be willing to offer a compromise to Colin rather than go to court. While Maude could attend this meeting as our friend, she would be unable to stand for us in court, as she was not yet qualified. She could recommend a colleague, but it would cost money. Although we had a small nest egg from the sale of the farm in Canada, expensive legal fees would reduce it and it would mean that Roddy's future would be less secure. It was a conundrum that needed the wisdom of Solomon.

The day of the meeting dawned bright and cold. Maude had arrived in North Uist the day before and had booked into the Lochmaddy Hotel rather than stay with us. She had invited us to dinner there that night, which was quite a treat for us, but unfortunately Colin Donaldson was there dining with the Laird who had come over to check on his estate so we were not comfortable. As we were leaving, he waved over to us and sniggered, no doubt enjoying our discomfort. After mother had arrived to help Morag look after the children, we set off to meet Maude at the hotel at 11 am. We then made our way to Mr Abernethy's office, which wasn't far from the Sheriff Court and within walking distance. My stomach was in knots and Roderick and I hardly said a word to one another.

Mrs Campbell's daughter, Rhona, was Mr Abernethy's secretary and she smiled brightly at us when we went into the office.

'Good morning, Chrissie. Good morning, Roderick. Mr Abernethy is expecting you. I'll just tell him you are here. Perhaps I could take your name Miss,' she said, looking at Maude.

'Maude Martin. I am a friend of Mr and Mrs Macdonald.'

She came back out and ushered us into Mr Abernethy's office. The walls were lined with shelves of thick law books covered in brown leather with red and green trim and gold lettering. There was a huge, polished mahogany desk surrounded by matching chairs with buttoned leather backs and cushions on which Mr Abernethy, Colin and another man were sitting. There was a roaring fire in the grate, which gave the room a welcoming feel and I wondered if Mr Abernethy was trying to lull us into a false sense of security.

'Good morning, Mr and Mrs Macdonald. Welcome. Please take a seat,' he said, after shaking our hands. 'And Miss Martin. I've heard of you. How are your studies going? Quite an honour being taken on by such a prestigious Glasgow practice.'

'Indeed. I am not yet qualified, so I am attending this meeting in the capacity of a friend of Mr and Mrs Macdonald, not as their solicitor.'

'Good, good. Let's get down to business then, shall we?'

I looked over at Colin and then at the man who was sitting by his side. There was something familiar about him and it was then I realised who he was. It was Frankie McNamara. So, he was the witness who Mr Abernethy had referred to in his letter. For some reason, I felt betrayed. Frankie had worked for us and we had treated him well. I thought he had been in love with Heather, so why would he support the man who had taken advantage of her?

Mr Abernethy shuffled papers around on his desk and then went into his drawer and took out his pipe. 'Don't mind if I smoke, do you ladies?'

'So long as you don't mind if I do too, Mr Abernethy,' said Maude, taking out a packet of cheroots.

'Oh, for God's sake man, just get on with it,' said Colin, 'stop wasting time.'

216

'Very well, Mr Donaldson,' he said, putting his pipe away mournfully. 'As I explained in my letter to you, Mr and Mrs Macdonald, Mr Donaldson claims he is the biological father of the boy known as Donald Ewen Macdonald. He has evidence to support this and Mr McNamara here is a witness to the birth of the said boy.'

'What exactly does Mr Donaldson want?'

'I want my son,' said Colin, moving forward in his chair. 'He's mine and I can prove it. You won't have a leg to stand on if I take you to court.'

'Mr Donaldson, Mr Donaldson, please calm down and let me do my job please.'

'When Mr Donaldson says he wants his son, Mr Abernethy, what precisely does he mean by that and what would he propose to do to legitimise the boy as his son?'

'My client proposes to apply for a new birth certificate for Donald Ewen Macdonald confirming he and his mother, Heather Macdonald, as the boy's natural parents. This would ensure that the boy would be registered as the legitimate heir to Mr Donaldson's estate when he dies. He would also request that the boy's name be changed to Colin Donald Donaldson.'

'No! You can't do that, Colin. You can't change his name. He's five years old. It would be too cruel to force him to change his name just for your gratification.'

'I'll do what I want, Chrissie Macdonald. Don't you forget where you come from and who your father rents his croft from.'

I shivered with fear. That threat of making my family homeless was too much, and I said no more. What a heartless bully he was. I could see the rage in Roderick's face and I'm sure Maude could too, as she intervened before Roderick could say anything.

'What evidence would Mr Donaldson use to prove his assertions?'

'I have here a list of the evidence which Mr Donaldson has in his possession. He hired a firm of private detectives in Canada who obtained this evidence and have provided signed affidavits to this effect.'

He handed over the following list.

1. A statement issued by Dr Angus Munro confirming that Roderick Macdonald suffered with consumption from 1912 to 1913 and that it was unlikely that he would have been in a fit condition to have marital relations with his wife, Christian Macdonald, at the time that the child known as Donald Ewen Macdonald was conceived.

2. A statement issued by Dr Angus Munro stating that the birth certificate he issued for the said child Donald Ewen Macdonald showed the mother as Heather Macdonald and the father as Colin Donaldson. He provided a duplicate copy of the certificate to the private detectives.

3. A certified copy of the said Donald Ewen Macdonald's Birth Certificate from Inverness County Council which states the parents as Christian and Roderick Macdonald signed by Dr Angus Munro. Dr Munro has signed an Affidavit to the effect that he did not issue such a certificate and that Mr and Mrs Macdonald must have stolen a sheet from his certificate book and forged his signature.

4. A copy of the death certificate of Heather Macdonald which states that she died in childbirth on the same date as the said Donald Ewen Macdonald was born.

5. Witness statements from Frankie McNamara and Hamish Fraser confirming that Colin Donaldson worked at the homestead of Roderick Macdonald during the period when the said child would have been conceived.

We were done for. He had all the evidence he needed to prove his case.

'May we have copies of these Affidavits Mr Abernethy, just for our records?' asked Maude.

'Of course. That won't be a problem. I had anticipated your request so the copies are in this envelope,' he replied, handing over a thick brown envelope.

'I think Mr and Mrs Macdonald need time to digest all this information, Mr Abernethy. May I suggest that since I am returning to Glasgow tomorrow, we break for lunch and reconvene again at 2.30 this afternoon.'

Mr Abernethy looked at Colin, who nodded his agreement with a smirk on his face. I looked at Frankie and couldn't help myself.

'And you Frankie, why on earth are you supporting this man?' I blurted out. 'You know what a scoundrel he is. You loved Heather; I cannot understand why you would take his side against us on this.'

'He saved my life in France, Mrs Macdonald. That's the long and the short of it.'

CHAPTER SIXTY-FOUR

We made our way to the hotel and Maude asked for sandwiches to be sent up to her room. We couldn't take the chance that Colin would be in the dining room and overhear our conversation.

'So, what do you think, Maude? Have we any chance of keeping Donald?' asked Roderick.

'I'll need to have a look at these papers he's given me,' she said, indicating the heavy envelope, 'but it looks as if he has sufficient evidence to back up his assertions that he and Heather are Donald's biological mother and father. However, that is only part of the story.'

'What do you mean?' I asked.

'Well, there is Donald's welfare to consider. What age is he now?'

'He's just turned five.'

'So, he is of an age where he identifies himself as Donald Macdonald and considers you and Roderick to be his mother and father. For him to have his name changed and be completely removed from your care would be detrimental to his well-being. In addition, you are the boy's biological grandfather, not some stranger who has no stake in the boy's welfare. Colin Donaldson has shown himself to be a dishonourable man in terms of his dealings with women and could be considered an unfit father for that reason.'

'But he had a distinguished career in the army and was severely injured whilst serving his country, so surely that would outweigh any harm he had caused Heather?'

'You're probably right Chrissie, so I think the best thing is to reach a compromise, making the argument that it would be detrimental to Donald to be taken away from you. We could argue that it would be in his best interests for you to keep custody and in exchange you would explain his true parentage to him and Colin would receive access rights until Donald reaches the age of sixteen when he can decide for himself who he would like to live with.'

'What do you think, Roderick? I hate the thought of having to tell Donald who his actual mother and father are, but I hate the thought of losing him altogether even more.'

'I doubt that Colin will accept the compromise, but it's worth a chance. It would distress Donald to be taken away from us and he would probably only end up in a boarding school in some godforsaken part of England.'

'It's important for me to know if you are prepared to go to court if Colin does not agree to our compromise. There's no point in offering a compromise without us having something that Colin would prefer didn't happen if he refuses.'

'I don't think we have a choice, Maude.'

'Right, let's get back and put our cards on the table.'

The meeting was a heated one and Colin completely lost his temper when we put our compromise to him, yelling at us that Donald was his son and he would live with him, no matter what.

'You can defend my action against you all you like, but you won't win. Remember who I am and who my father is. It would be a brave magistrate that would go against the Laird or his Factor.'

Leaving that threat hanging in the air, he stormed out of the meeting.

When we got home, we looked through the papers that Mr Abernethy had given Maude and which she had passed to us. I noticed that the copy of Heather's death certificate had been altered and that there was nothing that showed she was of native Canadian descent.

'What do you think that means, Roderick? Why would Colin have had Heather's death certificate amended?'

'Perhaps he is ashamed to own that Heather was half Cree. If that is the case, we have something to negotiate with him on. Perhaps his reputation is more precious to him than we think.'

CHAPTER SIXTY-FIVE

I wrote to Victoria asking for her help and was surprised when she told me she knew nothing of what Colin had been up to and neither did her father. She told me she would tell her father all that I had shared with her and that she was certain he would try to dissuade Colin from taking the action he was proposing. He did try. His father tried to convince him not to claim Donald as his son, arguing it would bring shame on the family. But when his father died shortly after this and Colin inherited his father's estate, it appeared at first that there was nothing and no one to convince him to do as his father had suggested. Mr Abernethy told us that he was therefore preparing the papers that would take the matter to court.

It was then I took matters into my own hands and made my way up to the Factor's house. Mrs McAllister was still there and made it as awkward as normal for me to gain entry. It was Colin himself who heard me at the door and told her to let me in.

'Well Chrissie. What brings you here? Have you decided to hand my boy over to me?' he said, with a smirk on his face.

'No Colin, I have not. I have come to appeal to your better nature. I believe you do have a better nature hiding somewhere inside you. You helped my brother Lachlan after all when you didn't need to.'

He looked at me and I thought I saw a flicker of something in his eyes and hoped that it was compassion.

'You claim to love Donald and yet you want to take him away from the people who have loved and cared for him since he was born. You also told me you loved Heather so, if that is true, do you think this is what she would want for her son?'

'I think she would love the thought of her son being part of the upper classes and having a good life rather than a crofter's son beholden to the local Laird.'

The smirk was back on his face.

'So, you are ready to let everyone know that your son is the child of a half-breed Cree squaw?'

I silently asked Heather to forgive me for using such language about her, but I hoped she would see that it was the only way that I might win the fight with Colin for her son. His face paled.

'What do you mean? There's no paperwork to suggest that his mother was a half-breed. I made sure of that.'

'Yes, I noticed the names on Heather's death certificate had been changed. But we have the original death certificate that Dr Munro issued with her full name on it – Heather Waskatamwi Macdonald – and the details of her parents, one of whom was a Cree woman. Roderick and I would also swear on oath, if you take us to court, that Heather was a half-breed Cree and who knows maybe Frankie would too.'

'Huh, your precious Roderick would condemn himself to ridicule and shame if he did that.'

'My precious Roderick, as you call him, would do anything for his grandson. He believes that loving someone occasionally means sacrifice, something you wouldn't understand.'

He said nothing, just stared at me, so I continued.

'I'll let you think about it Colin and you can have Mr Abernethy contact me when you have made your decision. The compromise we wish is firstly that you do not change Donald's Christian name and secondly that we keep custody of Donald until he reaches sixteen years when he will be mature enough to decide who he would like to live with. You will receive visiting rights which will give you access to him on every second weekend and he will spend the school holidays with you. In exchange, we will explain to Donald his parentage in as sensitive a way as we can and will not tell him of his native heritage.'

My heart was beating fast, but I said all this in as calm a voice as I could muster. I mustn't let him see how nervous I was. I turned on my heel and left the room without a backward glance. It was in God's hands now.

When I got home, Roderick asked me where I had been. I was uncertain how he would react, so felt relieved when he told me he approved of the action I had taken.

223

'Hopefully, the man will have some compassion for his son and agree to our proposal. We'll need to break the news to the boys. It's not something I'm looking forward to.'

'Me neither, but the sooner we do it, the better. Should we wait until we hear from Colin?'

'Yes. I think that's for the best.'

CHAPTER SIXTY-SIX

It didn't take long for Colin to instruct Mr Abernethy to come to an arrangement with us. He obviously did care what people thought of him after all. But the outcome was a compromise for us both. Roderick and I were no longer to have sole custody and responsibility for Donald. Instead, it was agreed that Roderick and I could have joint responsibility with Colin for Donald's upbringing, which meant he spent part of the week with us and part of the week with Colin. This arrangement was to stay in place until Donald reached sixteen when it was felt he could decide himself who he wished to live with. In exchange, Colin agreed to register Donald as his son and heir but agreed not to change his first name.

It was hard explaining to Colin who his natural mother and father were. We told him about Colin first and explained that it meant he would have wealth and status. We then took out Heather's photograph and showed it to him, explaining that she was his mother, not me. Donald took the picture and stared at it for a long time.

'She doesn't look like me and neither does that baby,' he said, throwing the picture on the floor. 'I don't want her to be my *mamaidh*. I want you *mamaidh*,' he said, crying and grabbing my hands. 'And I don't want a new *dadaidh*. I don't like that Colin. He wouldn't let me go when I saw him up at the big house.'

My heart was breaking as I saw the fear in his eyes and the sobs rending his little body and I did my best to comfort him.

But it wasn't just Donald who was upset by this change of circumstances. Roddy was also affected. We included him in the discussion with Donald, as we felt it was important that he knew and understood what was happening to his little brother. He was now nine, and I think understood better than Donald what was being said. When Roderick explained he was Donald's grandfather and not his father, Roddy at once interrupted him.

'Do you mean this Heather is my sister? She doesn't look like me. She looks funny. Where is she now?'

'She is your half-sister, Roddy. She had a different mother to you. Heather died when she had Donald and she is now in heaven.'

'So, Donald is going to become the Factor one day and if I become a crofter, he will be able to tell me what to do with my land?'

What could we say? It was true, but hopefully Roddy would be more than a crofter. We had as much ambition for him as Colin had for Donald. But the nub of the issue for Roddy was whether Roderick and I were his real parents or whether he was actually someone else's son.

'Are you and *mamaidh* my real father and mother or have you been pretending with me too?' he asked Roderick, his face a mask of fear and anger.

It took a long time for Donald to accept Colin as his father and to stay with him at the Factor's house, but Colin was genuinely fond of him and eventually he settled and for the two years that Colin lived, we managed to share Donald's care with good grace. We had to reassure Roddy constantly that he was our son and that no one would come to claim him or to take him away from us but I think he resented the times that Donald went to stay at the Factor's house and it created a tension between the two boys that had not been there before.

CHAPTER SIXTY-SEVEN

It is hard to believe all that has happened since Roderick and I became man and wife ten years ago. It would make an interesting story for a novel. I turn from Colin's coffin and gaze out the window at the grass blowing in the summer breeze. The wildflowers are out and the sea for once looks calm. It is beautiful. The Spanish flu epidemic had struck a war-weary country in 1918. As if we hadn't lost enough men and women to the war, God had to throw a flu epidemic at us. People were dropping like flies in the beginning, but we thought it was over now. Then, out of nowhere, it struck Colin down. Poor Colin. He had turned out to be a good and kind father to Donald.

Thanks to Maude, Colin's Will set up a Trust for Donald naming Roderick and me as his guardians if anything happened to him. I think of Maude and how she helped us throughout our fight for Donald for little financial reward and was glad that the government had changed the law and she could now practice as a solicitor. Life for women was changing little by little and now that I was thirty, I would be able to vote in parliamentary elections. The Trust is the reason that I will become mistress of the house where I used to work as a servant. I'm not sure how Mrs McAllister will take to me giving her orders, but I can't think about that now. I am saying my last goodbye to Colin before the undertaker closes the coffin and takes it away over the Minch to make its journey to Glasgow, where he will be buried next to his father.

Sitting on the sideboard is the photograph of Heather that we took when she had Donald. Colin had asked for it when he began bringing Donald to the house, and I was pleased that he had put it on display. Although her ancestry is not acknowledged, she is no longer a secret to be hidden and Donald's future is secure. When the Laird heard that we were Donald's guardians, he asked Roderick to take over the role of Factor for the island. I think how ironic that is. Knowing Roderick, he will do an excellent job of protecting the Laird's lands and game, but he will also show compassion for the men who take a little back from that land they and their ancestors suffered and died for. I think of Lachlan and hope that he is looking down on us from Heaven. I recently received confirmation from a publisher that they will print his poems, so he will always be remembered now.

The door opens and Roderick comes in.

'Are you ready Chrissie? The undertaker is waiting to close the coffin.'

'I'm ready Roderick,' I say, taking his hand. He looks at the photograph of Heather and smiles at me.

'She looks beautiful, doesn't she? I hope she's happy that a part of her is living on in North Uist. It would have pleased her to know that her son would one day become the owner of the Donaldson estate, don't you think?'

'I do, Roderick, I do.'

And as if they had heard us, the sound of our children's happy laughter reaches us from the garden.

The End

ACKNOWLEDGEMENTS

Writing **No Song in a Strange Land** has been a delight. I loved the research into that era and found out lots of things I didn't know. Most of my research was desktop and I am amazed at the information I was able to glean from the internet. However, I would like to mention two books that I found especially helpful.

The first is The Photographs of Archie Chisholm: Life and Landscapes in the Outer Hebrides 1818-1913 by Michael Cope and published by Thirsty Books. Mr Chisholm was the Procurator Fiscal on North Uist but he was also a photographer and chronicled the images of island life at that time. It allowed me to see how people dressed, what they worked at and what issues they faced.

The second is Farmer's Glory by AG Street and published by Faber and Faber. I obtained a copy on Amazon. AG Street went to Canada as a young man at the same time as my characters and worked in the Canadian Prairies, so much of what I discovered about farming and prairie living comes from this book.

I also used a cover designer for the first time on a site called Fiverr so thank you to Vickncharlie for their design.

My writing just seemed to flow which has meant the manuscript was ready to publish within a year, a record for me. I couldn't have done it without the help of special people in my life and I would like to thank them here.

My cousin, Marion, who filled me in on the details of my grandparents' time in Canada and about where they lived in North Uist.

My sister, Catherine, for her enthusiastic encouragement and commentary on my manuscript.

My readers, Liz, Margaret, Elizabeth, and Ian. Thank you for reading and making comments. As an author, I am sometimes too close to see the wood for the trees.

My husband, Charlie, for his continued support which has been unfailing since I began writing. He also booked lots of trips away in our campervan when lockdown was lifted, one of which was to North Uist as part of a Hebridean island hop. I was able to visit the places where my grandparents lived and to visit the cemetery where they are buried. It was a special experience and I loved the peaceful quiet beauty of the place.

I hope the people of North Uist don't mind me using their lovely island as the setting for this novel. Although my grandparents lived on the other side of the island, I decided to use Lochmaddy as the setting principally because when I visited this year, I was able to see the original post office that would have been in use at that time. I couldn't find out if there was a black house settlement close by so have used creative license in this part of my story.

I should also mention that I didn't know before I began my research that North Uist had its own war poet or that his most famous poem, the White Swan, is now a beautiful song sung by several famous Gaelic performers. If you get the chance look it up.

Finally, thank you for buying my book. I would love to hear what you think so would really appreciate if you could put a review on Amazon or Goodreads.

ABOUT THE AUTHOR

Marion developed an interest in creative writing when she retired from her job as director of a housing association and enrolled in a course with the Open University. She found she loved writing and began with short stories and poetry which she collected in **Wherever You Go** in 2021 for her husband Charlie's 70th birthday.

She then tried her hand at a novel. The result was **One Year** which she self-published in 2017. The Scottish Association of Writers awarded One Year second place in their competition for a self-published novel in March 2020. The judge said, 'The idea of this book grabbed me from the outset, and I found myself staying up late wanting to read just one more chapter – the sign of well-written page turner.'

Her second novel, **The Circle**, was published in August 2020 and she called it *an intriguing psychological novel with a twist.* As usual, contemporary issues supplied the backdrop to the story. In One Year, it was the financial crash and the refugee crisis, in The Circle it is coercive control and the #MeToo Movement. Both novels are available on Amazon in paperback and eBook.

She has now completed her third novel which she hopes to publish by the end of 2021. It is a historical novel set in North Uist and Canada during the period 1910 to 1920. She got the idea for the story when she did some research into her family tree.

She was born and educated in Scotland and lives in Glasgow with her husband, Charlie. Her interests include reading, travelling, scrabble, knitting, playing the ukulele and, of course, writing.

If you would like to keep up to date with Marion's writing journey, you can sign up for her blog posts at
http://marionmacdonaldindieauthor.wordpress.com

OTHER BOOKS BY THIS AUTHOR

ONE YEAR

When Suzie's husband, Andy, is killed while delivering aid in Syria, she is left devastated and virtually homeless. He had re-mortgaged their home to buy twenty properties in El Paraiso, an almost deserted golf resort in Spain, and she can't afford the repayments.

While in Spain trying to decide what to do with her legacy, she meets and is attracted to the mysterious Josh who appears to be living illegally in one of the apartments that Andy bought. To complicate matters, Andy's friend Ewan delivers a suitcase to Suzie and the contents suggest that Andy may have been involved in refugee smuggling.

Determined to uncover the truth, Suzie embarks on a journey of discovery, but what will the truth reveal?

One Year is an intriguing and emotional page-turner that keeps the reader guessing right up until the final chapter.

Buy on Amazon at https://amazon.co.uk/dp/B0785HGDVV

WHEREVER YOU GO

This book is a collection of the author's writing over the last seven years which she put together for her husband, Charlie, on his 70th birthday. It includes memoir/travel writing, flash fiction/short stories and poetry, most of which have not previously been published.

Buy on Amazon at https://amazon.co.uk/dp/B09BNSXMMS

THE CIRCLE

Something shocking happened to Debbie Halligan when she was fourteen.

Writing under the pen name of Jessica Aitken, she is now a successful author of crime novels set in Glasgow. On the outside she is confident and friendly but the legacy of neglect by alcoholic parents and the trauma she suffered at the age of fourteen have left their mark. Shortly after ending yet another relationship that hasn't worked for her, she joins a therapeutic knitting circle and embarks on a new affair, hoping this one might be different. Over the next few months, she is subjected to on-line bullying and blackmail, which drives her to self-soothe with alcohol and leaves her fearing for her sanity.

When a body is discovered bludgeoned to death in her apartment and she is nowhere to be found, the police must investigate if she too is a victim or if she is the perpetrator.

This psychological novel reflects how our actions can have consequences even after twenty-five years and cleverly knits together the connections of the characters in the book with Jessica's past. It takes place in the context of the contemporary issues of cyber bullying, coercive control and the #MeToo Movement.

Buy on Amazon at https://amazon.co.uk/dp/B08CVDP1N6

Printed in Great Britain
by Amazon

37789209R00138